Tommy Stands Tall

ROOSEVELT HIGH SCHOOL SERIES

Tommy Stands Tall

ROOSEVELT HIGH SCHOOL SERIES

Gloria L. Velásquez

PIÑATA BOOKS
ARTE PÚBLICO PRESS
HOUSTON, TEXAS

Tommy Stands Tall is made possible through a grant from the City of Houston through the Houston Arts Alliance.

Piñata Books are full of surprises!

Piñata Books
An imprint of
Arte Público Press
University of Houston
4902 Gulf Fwy, Bldg 19, Rm 100
Houston, Texas 77204-2004

Cover illustration and design by Vega Design Group

Printed in the United States of America
October 2013–November 2013
United Graphics, Inc., Mattoon, IL
12　11　10　9　8　7　6　5　4　3　2　1

For Aunt Dora, Uncle Archie and Bernie
Remembering Steve Joseph Quintana (1959-1996)

ONE
Tommy

Driving into the Laguna Heights neighborhood where Maya lives, I have to smile at her words yesterday. "Kick-ass seniors," that's what she called us. It seems like not too long ago I wondered if I'd ever get this far. And now, here I am, a kick-ass senior with my own car, anxiously waiting to hear if I've been accepted into San Francisco State. I guess I have changed. Maya once mentioned in my World Cultures class that in some Native American cultures, they believe people shed their skin like snakes, transforming themselves. Snake medicine. Maybe that's what I've done, shed my skin like Maya's snakes.

As soon as I ring the doorbell, the door is opened by Maya's mother. In her faded jeans and T-shirt, Professor Gonzales looks more like a student than a university professor. "Hello, Tommy," she says, inviting me inside as Maya instantly appears at her side. Although Maya insists she looks like her dad's side of the family, the resemblance to her mother is striking. The same olive skin and shiny black hair.

"Hey, Tomás," Maya says. "What movie are we seeing?"

This year Maya won't stop calling me by my Spanish name, even though I keep telling her it makes her sound as old as my mom. Maya claims it sounds more sophisticated now that we're almost college students.

"It's the new comedy with Manny Rodríguez."

"I've heard it's hilarious," Professor Gonzales comments. "How's your Mom, Tommy?"

I barely have time to utter a few words before Maya pushes me toward the doorway. "We have to run or we'll be late," she apologizes as I wave goodbye to Professor Gonzales. That's the thing about Maya that's always bothered me—she's always rushing to get things done. She could use some snake medicine herself.

"Nice wheels," Maya says, climbing into the front seat of my black Honda.

"Not as hot as yours," I reply, turning on the engine as we head toward downtown.

"Tomás, if it hadn't been for Mom and Dad's help, you know I couldn't have afforded my car."

"True," I agree, thinking about how Dad's always griping about every penny we spend. I don't know how Mom can take it. She clips coupons like crazy and is always shopping for bargains, but Dad still complains. When I get my college degree, I'm going to give Mom money so she can buy anything she wants, like that new bedroom set she's always talking about.

Maya's next remark pulls me back from my thoughts. "Tyrone had to go to some sort of indigenous drumming with the kids at the Teen Center."

"That's cool," I say, smiling to myself at Maya's attitude of superiority. This year she refers to anyone who is not a senior as a "kid." It really doesn't bother me. I know I'm damn lucky to have a friend like Maya who accepts me for who I am. It's hard to believe two years have gone by since that day when I tried to kill myself. Maya has stood by me through it all. She never once rejected me.

Arriving downtown, I find a parking space a few blocks from Main Street. We hurry over to the Rialto, but instead of going to the ticket booth, we go to the side entrance where my friend, Mark, is collecting the tickets. The moment he sees me, Mark waves us inside. "Awesome service," Maya teases, as we get in line at the snack bar.

After that, we find two empty seats in the middle row. While we munch on popcorn, the theater begins to fill. "Isn't that the new Chicano at Roosevelt?" Maya whispers, pointing to the curly-haired student walking down the aisle with another guy who doesn't look familiar.

"Yeah, his name's Albert. He's from some place called Tracy, wherever that is."

My mind drifts to the first time I saw Albert. It was at the school library and he was telling the librarian, the Amazon Queen, that he had just moved to Laguna with his parents, that he had an older sister who was studying back East. Later that same day, I'd run into Albert in the hallway. Although we never spoke, we stared at each other for the longest time and I felt an odd connection with him.

When the lights are suddenly dimmed, my attention focuses back on the screen. After almost ten minutes of commercials and previews, the movie finally begins. Manny Rodríguez, the most popular Latino comedian today, is playing the role of Billy, the Barrio Funeral Planner who hauls coffins around in the back of his SUV. Billy goes from house to house with his shiny Virgen de Guadalupe bumper stickers, giving huge discounts to all his *compadres* and homeboys in East LA. By the time the movie ends, Maya and I have laughed our guts out.

As we file out of the crowded theater, I catch a glimpse of Albert and his friend moving toward one of the exits. Once we are standing outside in the street, Maya asks, "Want to go to Yo Yo's for some yogurt?"

Shaking my head, I explain, "Sorry, I can't. I've got loads of homework for tomorrow."

"You need to lighten up, Tomás—it's our senior year!"

"I know, but I want to make sure I'm well-prepared for San Francisco State."

"Don't be a *tonto*—you'll be more than ready," Maya says, as we turn and start walking back to the car.

Sometimes I wish I had Maya's confidence, but the reality is that I don't have college-educated parents like she does. Dad works nights as a custodian at Laguna Hospital, while Mom cleans houses all day. Things have never come easy in *my* family.

After I drop Maya off at her house, I drive back to the apartment. Dad is in the living room watching the evening news with Mom. I know he isn't working tonight since he is wearing one of his lame plaid shirts. "How was the movie?" Mom asks, glancing up from the couch.

"Funny—Manny Rodríguez is the new Cantinflas. You'd like him."

Dad's unexpected question takes me by surprise. Without taking his eyes off the TV, he asks, "Tomás, can I borrow your car tomorrow? My battery's dead."

Hesitating, I answer, "I guess so. I can catch a ride to school with Tyrone."

I wait for a thank you that never comes. Frustrated, I head upstairs to my room, thinking about how my relationship with Dad sucks, but at least he isn't ignoring me anymore. At least now he asks me for help, even though he still pretends I'm not gay. We never talk about it; never mention it. Like Maya once said when she was talking about how people still stare at her and Tyrone, we can't change the world overnight.

I'm almost finished with my Math homework, when the door opens and María, the older of my two sisters, suddenly appears in my room. María turned eleven year this year and we get along fairly well, but she still gets on my nerves sometimes, especially when she tries to boss nine-year-old Amanda around. Mom once told me she thinks María's jealous because Amanda has green eyes and is *güerita* like me, while María looks more like Mom's side of the family. "You're supposed to be asleep!" I gently scold her, as Amanda's little head pops through the cracked door.

"You too, *gordita!*" I add, ordering them to bed. "You both have school tomorrow and if Dad finds out you're still awake, you're in for trouble."

Pushing Amanda out of the room, a disappointed María says, "Okay, but can I borrow your Lonely Boys CD? "

"Maybe tomorrow," I answer, wishing María weren't acting so damn pre-teeny. "Now go to bed."

The last thing I hear as the door shuts behind them is Amanda's sweet little voice whispering good night.

TWO

Monday morning, I am standing at my locker when Maya comes walking up to me with Juanita and Ankiza at her side. "Did you hear the news last night?" she asks as I close the locker door, stuffing my books in my backpack.

"Are you kidding? I never watch the local news—they suck."

"A high school student was badly beaten and taken to the hospital."

"Oh yeah? I wonder who it was."

Juanita is quick to reply, "I'm sure we'll know before the day is over with all the *chismosos* at Roosevelt."

"Girl, you know that," Ankiza agrees, as we move through the crowded hallway.

Before they exit the building, Maya says, "See you at noon, Tomás. Don't forget we're meeting in front of the gym."

Pre-calculus is definitely my favorite class this year. Mr. Adams always calls on me to go to the chalkboard and work out a problem. At first, I used to get embarrassed, but after a while I realized it was fun showing off with something I've loved since elementary school.

Today is my lucky day. Mr. Adams has us work in pairs the entire hour, which is cool because I'm paired up with

Molly, who is another smart math person like me. We finish the problems way ahead of the other students, so we spend the rest of the period playing chess in the corner of the room. I once thought chess was only for white people, but now I know that's not true. One day, I'd like to teach Amanda and María how to play it.

My second period is Senior English. Writing has never been one of my strengths and this semester we're working on literary compositions. Mine is on Langston Hughes, one of the greatest African-American writers of all time. Maya once gave me a poster that I still have on my bedroom wall that reads, *Hold fast to dreams, for if dreams die, life is a broken winged bird that cannot fly.* I didn't know then that they were verses from a poem by Langston Hughes.

I am printing out the first draft of my essay when I overhear two students behind me commenting on last night's news bulletin. "I heard it was that new sophomore, Albert, in the hospital," Jason explains.

"That's what I heard too," Brittany says. "Poor guy—guess he was hurt badly."

I can still picture Albert with his friend at the Rialto, looking relaxed and content. Pretending I need another copy, I linger a while longer waiting to see if Jason and Brittany say anything else, only they don't. The conversation switches to senior night and I'm left wondering if Albert is all right.

By lunch time, the news that it was Albert who was badly beaten spreads throughout the campus. When I meet up with Maya, Juanita and Rudy at the gym, Maya tells me, "They're saying it was Albert. Isn't it weird that we just saw him last night at the movies?"

Rina, who walks up at that exact moment with Ankiza at her side, says, "It was Albert all right. He's in my Spanish class, but he wasn't there today."

"I heard it happened at Tomol Beach, that he was with another guy," Rudy states, as we walk toward the parking lot.

"So? What's wrong with that?" I ask defiantly, glaring at Rudy.

Defending himself, Rudy states, "I didn't mean anything by that. I'm only saying he wasn't alone."

"Chill out, Tommy," Rina interrupts. "Rudy might be a *mosco,* but he's cool."

Thinking I might have overreacted, I mumble an apology to Rudy. After all, he has changed his way of thinking over the years. As we hurry to our cars, so we can get to and from Burger King before lunch period ends, I manage to push Albert out of my thoughts.

After lunch, I go to my computer CAD class. This is my final class of the day since I'm enrolled in job experience and work at the Rialto during sixth period. This semester we're designing a small house with two floors. I've always liked to draw, so it's even more fun doing it on the computer. Mr. Giles lets us mess around a lot in class. Sometimes I even draw superheroes like Batman in his twenty-first-century Batmobile. I like to imagine it's me with all the superpowers eliminating all the bad guys.

As soon as fifth period ends, I head out to my car. Pulling out of the parking lot, I make an unexpected decision. Instead of driving toward the theater, I turn in the direction of General Hospital. I'm not sure what compels me to do this, but the next thing I know, I'm at the reception desk inquiring about Albert's room number. Within seconds, I'm on the elevator, pushing the button for the third floor.

When I arrive at Albert's room, I pause for a moment, flooded with the memory of waking up in a hospital room, feeling desperate and afraid, after they'd pumped my stomach. Sucking my breath in, I chase away the dark images before I open the door to go inside.

Albert eyes widen in surprise when he sees me enter the room. He's propped up against a pillow, watching music videos. "What are you doing here?" he asks, tinges of sarcasm in his voice.

Moving closer to his bedside, I notice that Albert's top lip is purple and swollen. His left eye is badly bruised and he has a cut with several stitches above his right eye. "I heard what happened. Can I sit down?"

"Suit yourself," Albert mumbles, pretending to focus his attention back on the TV screen.

"We've never met, but my name's Tommy—Tommy Montoya."

Albert turns to look at me, his eyes blazing like wildfires. "I know who you are. What do you want?"

Shifting uncomfortably in my seat, I answer, "I wondered if I could help, that's all." There are tiny little needles pricking my neck and shoulders. Maybe this wasn't a good idea after all. Maybe I shouldn't have come.

Wincing as if he is in pain, Albert says, "I don't need any help. I'm fine. It was all a misunderstanding, that's all. You can go now."

Taking a deep breath, I tell him, "I'm here because I wanted you to know that you have a friend—a friend you can trust."

Albert's gaze is on me again and I recognize the fear in his eyes, the desperate plea for help. "Why should you care?" he blurts out. "Besides, how do I know I can trust you?"

"Because you can, that's why."

Albert is suddenly quiet and I'm certain he is experiencing the same connection I'd felt when I first saw him at Roosevelt. After a moment or two, Albert begins to speak in a low voice, "We weren't doing anything. My friend J.J. and I were just sitting next to each other at the beach talking. Then these skinhead looking guys going by stopped to ask us for a light—they were drunk. When I told them we didn't have any matches, the big husky one said, "Are you two homos?"

"When the other guys snickered, I knew we were in real trouble. Then one of them said, 'He's nothing but a beaner.' Then they started to laugh hard and I felt my blood start to boil, so I stood up and said, 'Who are you calling a beaner?' That's when they lunged forward and while the two of them held me back, the husky guy began to beat the crap out of me. The next thing I remember is being in the emergency room."

"What about your friend? Is he all right?"

Nodding, Albert explains, "J.J. said he wanted to jump in and stop them, but they threatened him to stay out of it. He's the one who called 911."

I am about to ask another question when a slim, dark-haired woman abruptly walks into the room. She is wearing a pin-striped Armani suit that makes her appear as if she has just stepped out of *Fortune 500*. Glancing at me, she says, "Al, sweetie, I didn't know you had company." Then, she looks my way again, saying, "I'm Al's mother. Now who may I ask are you?"

Her brash, direct manner takes me by surprise. "I'm Albert's friend, Tommy," I answer, as she shifts her gaze back to Albert, who seems agitated by his mother's unexpected appearance.

"Al sweetie, the police officers said that if you can identify the persons who did this to you, we can press charges."

"Mom, I told you I don't want to do that," Albert insists. "All they took was twenty bucks, it's not worth it."

When Albert's mother launches into a fervent argument about why it is prudent to file charges against the alleged suspects, I decide it's time to leave. "I have to go. Here's my cell phone number," I carefully interrupt, handing Albert a small scrap of paper.

"Thanks, dude," Albert whispers as his mother flashes me a phony smile that matches her appearance.

As I exit the hospital room, I can hear them arguing intensely. It is crystal clear that Albert has lied to his parents, making it seem like it was a mugging. That's how it all begins, I think to myself, pressing the button for the elevator. One lie after another. Lies that never seem to end. Welcome to the club, Albert.

THREE

The next few days at school, the rumors about Albert get uglier. On Thursday, I've just come out of CAD class and I'm stooped down at the water fountain, when I hear Michael Stein, Roosevelt's star quarterback telling two of his friends, "That guy Albert's a fag, that's what I think." They all start to laugh, but their smiles fade the moment they notice me.

Taking a few steps toward Michael, I ask accusingly, "Who are you calling a fag?"

Michael's face turns crimson, but he doesn't back down. Glaring right back at me, he says, "Don't tell me you're one of them, too?"

My heart is pounding like a jack hammer. Michael weighs twice as much as I do and with all those muscles, he could smash me like a *cucaracha*. But I don't let that stop me. I lean into him, our faces inches apart. I can see the tiny beads of perspiration forming on his forehead. "And what if I am?"

Just then, there is a firm yank on my arm and I turn around to face Maya, who pulls me away toward the nearest exit. "Are you crazy, Tomás?" she says, raising her voice above the sound of the tardy bell. "Michael could've hurt you badly."

"So?" I reply sarcastically, as we exit the building and find a quiet place on an empty bench.

"Tomás, you could get in trouble for fighting, then you wouldn't graduate. What brought all of that on anyway?"

Frustrated, I recount the entire incident to Maya and when I'm finished, she says, "Everyone knows Michael's an idiot. Besides, he's not the only bigot at Roosevelt, or in the entire world for that matter."

Although I know Maya is right, I'm suddenly sick of it all. "Well, he and all those other homophobes deserve a good beating."

Now Maya's face becomes rigid like stone, her brown eyes drilling into me. "Tomás, that's not the way to change attitudes and you know it."

"Yeah, I know. I shouldn't have let Michael get to me. But they were bad-mouthing Albert and I couldn't stand it."

"Have you talked to Albert any more since that day at the hospital?"

I shake my head. "I gave him my cell number, but he hasn't called me. I hate that everyone's talking about him."

Maya pats me gently on the arm, if anyone understands me, it's her. After all, Maya was the first person I came out to and if it hadn't been for her calling my mom that day, I might be dead right now. Rising slowly to my feet, I say, "I'm due at the Rialto. But thanks for saving my butt."

Maya smiles. "Remember, Tomás, I'm here for you. Call me later."

By the time I arrive at the Rialto, I'm somewhat relaxed and able to concentrate on getting the theater ready for the Thursday night bargain shows. Kyle, who is the manager, orders me to get the popcorn machine going and to restock the candy supplies. He then sends Mark and I up and down the theater rows making sure all the trash has been picked up. This is one duty I really dislike, but hey, a job's a job. Sometimes I get to work at the ticket counter, which is what I like the most since I'm able to use my math skills, even if it is in a minor way; however, it makes me very uncomfortable when someone I know from Roosevelt expects me to let them in free. It's one thing for me to get in free once in a while like I did with Maya the other night, but those other bums don't even work here.

The theater fills up quickly tonight, mostly with college students. The movie is about a comical love triangle between this guy, his internet girlfriend and his best friend. Watching a few scenes from the movie, I'm reminded of Mom's *telenovelas*. Flashy and fake, that's what I think, feeling relieved when the movie finally ends. After I help Mark clean up the theater for the next show, I get ready to leave.

Mom is lying on the couch, half-asleep when I get home. She is wearing the flowery pink pajamas we gave her for Christmas and the black hair net she always wears at bedtime. Mom always waits up for me. Juanita says her Mom does the same thing, that she always waited for Carlos when he lived at home. The minute she notices me, Mom asks, "How was work, *hijo*?"

Sinking into Dad's favorite armchair, I say, "It was busy. Dad's not home yet?"

"*Ya mero, hijo.*" There is a slight pause, then Mom continues, "I heard on the news about the student who got beat up from your school. Do you know who it was?"

Ever since that awful year, Mom's intuition is razor sharp as if she can sense what's on my mind. Not Dad. He's like a living corpse, absolutely clueless about my life. "Yeah," I mutter, wondering if I should confide in Mom, tell her about Albert.

After a very long moment, I gaze into Mom's eyes. The gentleness and understanding in her tired face remind me that I can trust her, that Mom has always been on my side. Within seconds, I find myself describing my visit to Albert in the hospital. I also tell Mom all about the confrontation with that idiot, Michael, at school today.

When I finally pause, Mom says, "*Hijo*, I'm so glad Maya showed up when she did. Getting into a fight could've ruined all your plans. Maya's right to tell you that there will always be people around who are narrow-minded."

"I know, but I don't want Albert to go through what I did. Everyone's bad-mouthing him." Pausing, I add, "I think Albert's gay but he's afraid to come out. I wish I could help him."

"Why don't you ask Doctora Martínez for her advice? Remember how much she helped us?"

My thoughts are suddenly clear. No wonder they say Moms are the smartest persons in the family. Why didn't I think of Ms. Martínez? On my feet, I say, "Yeah, maybe— thanks, Mom," then I give her a kiss on the forehead as I head for the stairway.

Upstairs in my room, I dial Maya's number on my cell phone. "Aren't you asleep yet, Tomás?" Maya answers, sounding perky and wide-awake even though it's almost midnight.

"I just got back from the Rialto. Listen, I was talking to Mom about Albert and she mentioned Ms. Martínez. Mom thinks I should get her advice about Albert."

"Your mom must be some kind of Houdini. I was thinking the exact same thing."

"So you think it's a good idea?"

"*¡Órale!*" Maya quickly agrees, sounding just like Juanita.

"I won't have time to call Ms. Martínez tomorrow because Fridays are super busy at the Rialto."

"If you want, I'll call her for you. Maybe Ms. Martínez can see you on Saturday. Listen, I have to go—Mom just banged on my door."

Hanging up, I realize why Mom is always reminding me that Maya *is* the best friend I've ever had.

FOUR
Ms. Martínez

For the past two Saturdays, I'd gone into my office to see clients, but not today. Instead, I had lounged around in my pajamas until almost eleven, then gone on my weekend hike without Frank. It seemed like ever since he had joined the new accounting firm, he was spending more time at the office. Still, it was my turn to be patient. When I'd started my practice last year, my days had been filled with long hours establishing my new clientele.

I was in the backyard watering my rosebushes when I heard the doorbell ring. Walking around to the front of the house, I found Tommy standing on the front steps. His wavy hair was cut shorter, making his face look fuller. His green eyes sparkled with confidence. "Perfect timing, " I said, inviting him into the living room.

"Everything looks the same," Tommy said, taking a seat on the couch.

"I'll take that as a compliment. Where's Maya?"

"I thought I'd come by myself, if that's okay."

"Of course it is," I answered, wondering what Tommy needed to see me about. Maya had been evasive on the phone.

Leaning forward, Tommy said, "I really need your advice, Ms. Martínez. There's this new guy at school, Albert, and I don't know him very well, but he was badly beaten by some idiots. You might've heard about it on the local news. Anyway, I went to see Albert at the hospital and I tried to talk to him about it." Tommy paused, taking a deep breath. "I think Albert's gay, but he's afraid to talk about it, and now there are all kinds of rumors going around. Albert's become the focus of every anti-gay joke at Roosevelt. When I saw him at the hospital, I gave him my phone number, but he still hasn't called me."

Now I understood why Tommy was here. He was afraid for Albert, that something bad might happen, that he might attempt to take his own life as Tommy had once done. My thoughts suddenly raced to my brother, Andy. The tragic accident, all the unanswered questions. Could Andy have been hiding his own secret?

"I feel so helpless," Tommy sighed, bringing me back from the past. "I don't know how to help Albert."

"I think you've already helped Albert by letting him know he has a friend he can trust. But remember, Tommy, the coming out process can take a long time and it's different for every person."

"I know, it's just that I want to help Albert."

Hoping to ease Tommy's concern, I gently explained. "I think Albert will talk to you when he's ready. Do his parents know?"

"I don't think so. That also worries me."

"I'm sure it does. Albert will have to decide for himself if and when he's ready to tell his family. You know that, Tommy."

He was quiet for a moment as he stared out the window. I knew he was reflecting on his relationship with his own parents and their strong reactions when they'd finally found out he was gay. It had been explosive and hurtful for the entire family, especially for Tommy.

Interrupting his silence, I went on, "The best thing you can do right now is to be Albert's friend. He needs all your support, especially at school." A sudden thought struck me. "Tommy, you once mentioned forming a gay and lesbian student organization at Roosevelt. That would be an excellent source of support for your friend, as well as for raising awareness at Roosevelt."

Tommy was pensive. "I've always thought about doing it, except now, I'm graduating and it might be too late. Besides, I wouldn't have the first clue about how to get one started."

"It's never too late, and all the information you need is online. You can do a search for schools that have founded similar organizations. As a matter of fact, you might want to start with Fairfax High School in LA. It was one of the first schools in the country to start a Gay Straight Alliance Club."

Tommy eyes widened with excitement. "I might just do that. Thanks for the advice, Ms. Martinez."

"You're very welcome. Let me know if I can help in any way."

After Tommy left, I went into the bedroom which served as my office, to catch up on my paperwork. As soon as I heard Frank's car pull into the driveway, I went out to meet him in the living room. Despite being married for all these years, my heart still fluttered at the sight of Frank, with his good looks and those Paul Newman eyes.

Giving me a quick kiss on the lips, Frank asked, "What's for dinner? I'm starved."

It seemed like Frank had the appetite of a teenager. He was constantly hungry, no matter how much he consumed. Smiling, I answered, "I thought I'd make your favorite dish—enchiladas."

"Good, because my *panza* is growling," he answered, sitting on his favorite end of the couch. "How was your afternoon?"

"Interesting. Tommy came by—he needed some advice about one of his friends. Remember the breaking news the other night about a student who was beaten? It turns out it was a friend of Tommy's."

"Really?"

"Yes. His name is Albert and Tommy thinks he might be gay. He's worried for him."

"Tommy has every reason to be concerned. Remember the Matthew Shephard story? How those idiots in Wyoming killed him just because he was gay?"

Nodding quietly, I thought back to the murder of Matthew Shephard in 1998, and how it had made international headlines. Matthew Shephard was a twenty-two-year-old political science major and, according to news reports, after leaving a bar in the company of two men, he was tied to a fence, beaten and left for dead in freezing temperatures. He was found eighteen hours later by two passing motorists who thought he was a scarecrow from the way he had been pinned on the fence. The Matthew Shephard murder trial made international headlines and became the focus of the largest anti-gay murder trial in U.S. history. As a result, Matthew Shephard quickly became a symbol for gay rights groups throughout the country, who demonstrated and voiced a need for the adoption of hate crime legislation.

Interrupting my thoughts, Frank asked, "So what's Tommy planning on doing?"

"Well, I'm not sure, but one of my suggestions was that he follow through on his idea of founding a Gay Straight Alliance Club at Roosevelt."

"That's a great idea. Bryan once told me he wished he'd had a club like that in high school, that it was pure hell keeping it a secret that he was gay when he was a teen."

Secrets, I repeated in my head. Secrets that eventually ruined people's lives. "I know Brian would agree that a GSA is an excellent support system for gay and lesbian youth. And if anyone can make this happen at Roosevelt, it's Tommy. He's stronger, more self-assured now, and I think he's ready for the challenge."

That was all Frank needed to jump to his feet and flex his muscles, exclaiming, "*The Amazing Race*—I can meet the challenge!"

Chuckling at Frank's silliness, I gave him a playful swig on his stomach, saying, "Come on, *panzón*. You can flex your muscles with the cheese grater."

FIVE
Ms. Martínez

I awakened Sunday morning feeling as if I were back home in Delano, but I soon realized it was only a dream. My brother, Andy, and I had been playing in Mr. Jamison's apple orchards, where my father had once worked. Images of Andy filtered through my mind, his sandy-colored hair pasted to his forehead from the sun's heat as he impishly challenged me to catch him. At the end of the dream, I was frantically searching for Andy, hurrying to see if the body lying on the side of the road belonged to him.

My heart felt heavy as I went to my closet to search for the familiar blue album. I spent the next few minutes in bed gazing at pictures of Andy. His first communion. His first bike. I paused when I came to the picture of Andy standing next to Tony, his best friend in high school. My mind went back to the last time I had seen Tony. It was right after Andy's funeral. I'd asked Tony if he knew why Andy would take his own life, that I didn't believe what the police report stated about Andy being high on cocaine when his car had crashed into the electrical pole. Tony was evasive, insisting he didn't know anything. Still, the uneasiness in his voice made me feel as if he were holding something back.

My eyes blurry, I continued going through the pictures, pausing at a photo of Andy and I sitting at the kitchen table playing a game of chess. That year, Andy had discovered his love of chess. Closing my eyes for a moment, I remembered the last time I'd talked with Andy. I was away at college and I'd called home. Andy had answered the phone and when I asked him about his chess game, he said he wasn't playing much. I'd then teased him about finding a hot date for the annual Homecoming Dance, only Andy had confessed he wasn't going. His next question had taken me by surprise. "Sandy, do you think you can come this weekend?" At the time, I hadn't thought anything of Andy's unexpected request, but now I realized there had been urgency in his voice. Andy had wanted to talk to me about something important that he couldn't discuss over the phone. My mind flashed back to the time I'd run into Andy with a male friend on one of the hiking trails at Laguna park. Andy had seemed unusually nervous when I'd asked him to introduce me to his friend.

Frank's voice jolted me back to the present. "Morning, hon," he said handing me my morning cup of coffee and the *LA Times*. "Are you looking at those pictures again?"

Frank was always the first one out of bed on Sunday mornings; he still spoiled me with coffee in bed. "Thanks, hon," I answered. "I couldn't help it. I had this awful dream about Andy last night."

"Oh, I'm sorry."

My voice barely audible, I admitted, "Frank, there's something I've never voiced out loud. I'm starting to wonder if Andy was gay and that was why he killed himself."

Frank squinted. "Are you serious?"

"I've been thinking about this since Andy's friend, Tony, came to see me."

Just then, we were interrupted by the jingling of a telephone. "It's mine," Frank said. "I left it on the kitchen table," and then he was gone from the room.

In an attempt to distance myself from my thoughts about Andy, I focused my attention on the day's headlines. The article on the increasing U.S. casualties in Iraq were depressing, so I turned to the Calendar section. I was immersed in an article on Culture Clash's new play at the Mark Taper Forum when Frank returned. "That was Diego. Bryan's in the hospital again."

"What happened?" I asked, wishing I could erase the worry lines on Frank's finely sculpted forehead.

"Pneumonia," Frank explained, sitting on the edge of the bed. "He's fine, but they're giving him IVs and more pills, according to Diego."

"I'm so sorry. Do your mom and dad know?"

"Bryan insisted Diego keep quiet about it, so he hasn't called them yet, but if I know Mom, she'll figure it out soon."

Bryan had successfully lived with HIV for almost a decade now. Still, it seemed like lately he was in and out of the hospital more often. We all knew he was battling an incurable disease. "Are you going to see him?"

"Diego said to hold off, for me to call Bryan tomorrow."

Diego was one of those living angels Mom always talked about. He had been Bryan's devoted partner for many years now and without him, I don't know how Bryan would have endured all this time.

I reached out to caress Frank's hand. "Sweetheart, I'm so sorry. I know how hard this is on your family."

"It's hardest on Mom," Frank said, bowing his head. After a quiet moment, he looked up, asking, "Now, what was that you were saying about Andy being gay?"

"I don't know for sure if Andy was gay. It's only a suspicion."

"Hon, you really need to think this through carefully before coming to that conclusion. It could hurt a lot of people."

"Yes, I know. I need to talk to Mom first. If anyone knows the truth, it would be her. Forget Dad—he was always drinking. Only I'm not sure how to approach the subject with Mom. She never talks about Andy's death, and you know how strained our relationship has always been."

"Be careful, Sandy," Frank warned. "This can either bring you and your mom closer together or it can drive you further apart."

"Yes, I know," I said, reaching up to stroke his cheek. I was taken aback when Frank abruptly stood up, saying he had to get back to the Sport Section. He disappeared from my side, leaving me bewildered.

As I rose from the bed and went into the bathroom to shower, I wondered if the news about Bryan was upsetting Frank more than he wanted to admit. My thoughts switched back to Andy. Frank was right. I needed to be cautious, especially with my parents. Dad had been sober for almost a year now and his relationship with Mom was better than ever. Still, I needed to find out the truth once and for all. It was something I needed to do out of love for Andy and for our family. Maya Angelou's verses suddenly appeared in my head: *Love costs all we are and will ever be. Yet it is only love which sets us free. A brave and startling truth.*

SIX
Tommy

I'm rushing to beat the third-period tardy bell, when I run right smack into Albert. I say hello to him, only he walks past me without a word as if he hasn't seen me. I'm tempted to turn around and go after him, but on second thought, I keep quiet. Albert already has enough to confront since his return to Roosevelt. Although the rumors have subsided, students continue to stare and gossip behind his back, just like they did with me that year. It's an awful feeling, that's for sure.

This year in Advanced Spanish, we're reading best-selling novels in Spanish and writing analytical essays. I really like Mr. Villamil because he never disrespects us when we use words like *plogear* and *wáchale*. He simply smiles, then he gives us the standard Spanish word. Sometimes Mr. Villamil repeats other Spanish words, derived from English, that they use in his native country of Puerto Rico, words like *biles* for bills. He likes it when I tell him Mom uses that word all the time.

Today's discussion turns out to be interesting since it focuses on the chapter in *Bendíceme Última* where Última, the *curandera*, cures one of Antonio's uncles, who has been bewitched by the evil Trementina sisters. Several Latino students share funny stories about how their grandma cured someone in their family who had *mal de ojo*. When Jean Ornelas describes in detail how one of her aunts used a raw egg to cure her cousin from *mal de ojo*, the Anglo students start to freak out. I have to laugh at them. Ever since I can remember, Mom has used her own silly *remedios* every time one of us gets sick. The raw egg thing doesn't scare me at all.

As the bell rings and we file out of class, I catch up to Jean Ornelas. "That was cool about your aunt," I say, adding, "Can I talk to you for a few minutes?"

"Yeah, sure, but make it quick—I'm off to the library to see the Amazon Queen."

Moving to the side of the hallway where we can talk without being trampled on, I begin. "I'm thinking of starting a Gay Straight Alliance Club. I've been doing some online research, so I was wondering if you'd like to help."

Her eyes widening, Jean says, "You know, I've been thinking about the exact same thing. I almost ripped Leon's ugly face apart when he called me a lesbo the other day in class."

I've always admired Jean for her openness about being a lesbian. I remember when I first met her during Freshman year. That was one of the first things she mentioned and, although I was shocked to hear her say this so openly, I didn't let on. During that awful year, Jean was one of the few friends like Maya that I knew I could count on. The weird thing is we've never really sat down and talked about being gay. I wonder if her parents know she's a lesbian.

"Dumbass Leon," I quickly agree. "There's so much ignorance at Roosevelt. That's why I thought of forming the club, especially before we graduate."

"Well, you can count me in!" Jean fervently states. "The first we'll need to do is find an advisor for our club."

"I've already thought about that. I was thinking of Mr. Miller. He's always been supportive of diversity issues."

"*Órale*," Jean enthusiastically agrees. "Why don't we go see him at lunch time? He's usually in his classroom."

"Good idea. I'll meet you by my locker after fourth period."

✳ ✳ ✳

At lunchtime, Jean is waiting at my locker. As we head for the Math building, I admit that I'm anxious about the best way to approach Mr. Miller. "Don't worry," Jean reassures me. "Mr. Miller's cool."

Mr. Miller is sitting at his desk grading papers and the minute he sees us walk through the doorway, he says, "What's up? Need some tutoring?" His pale blue eyes widen as he waits for an answer.

"Don't look at me, Mr. Miller. I got a passing grade on my last test, and you know Tommy's a math genius."

Mr. Miller smiles, motioning for us to take a seat. Clearing my throat, I begin, "Jean and I are thinking of starting a Gay Straight Alliance Club at Roosevelt."

Before I can continue, Jean jumps in to say, "And we were wondering if you'd like to be our advisor."

Mr. Miller hesitates. "Well, it's a little late in the school year . . . " Then, pausing for a brief moment, he adds, "But

I think it's a very good idea. And yes, I'd be glad to be your advisor."

Jean and I glance at each other, satisfied, while Mr. Miller continues. "The first thing we'll need to do is fill out a charter for the club. I can get the necessary forms, then we can meet to go over them. How soon were you planning on holding the first club meeting?"

"The sooner the better," Jean answers, and I nod in complete agreement.

"If I'm right, you can go ahead and hold unofficial meetings until the charter is approved. Let me find out about that."

"Thanks, Mr. Miller," we repeat in unison as the warning bell rings for fifth period.

Hurrying back to my locker for my books, I meet up with Maya, Rudy and Juanita, who are returning from lunch.

"Where were you, Tomás?" Maya asks. "We waited for you, but you never showed, so we went to Foster Freeze without you."

"I was with Jean. We went to talk with Mr. Miller about starting a Gay Straight Alliance Club."

"It's about time," Maya says. "You can count me in."

"Good. We'll definitely need help in spreading the word, as well as recruiting members."

When Juanita eagerly states that she also wants to join the club and help out in any way she can, Rudy gives her a slight nudge on the side, but Juanita refuses to back down, telling him, "You can join, too, if you want."

Insisting he's late for class, Rudy shrugs his shoulders and disappears down the hallway before I can tell him what I think of his rude behavior.

Maya turns to me and says, "Don't let Rudy get to you."

"Yeah, he's an insecure *tonto*," Juanita admits.

"Roosevelt really needs a Gay Straight Alliance Club. I'm proud of you for doing this."

"Thanks," I tell Maya as she and Juanita hurry off down the hallway to their next class.

At my locker, I'm still pissed about Rudy's attitude. That idiot is probably worried other students might think he's gay if he associates with the club. There's a lot of stupid people who think like that. *Ni modo*, I repeat out loud. That's their problem.

SEVEN

Once we've reviewed and signed the charter form for our new club, Mr. Miller turns them into the ASB office. After that, Jean and I prepare the flyer announcing our first informational club meeting for the following Tuesday. We post them throughout campus and by the end of the week, the word is out about the Gay Straight Alliance Club. When we find some of the flyers crumpled up on the floor, Jean simply shrugs her shoulders, saying, "You watch—this is only the beginning." She then carefully puts up several new flyers where the old ones hung.

I'm coming out of CAD class when I spot Albert at the water fountain. Moving to his side, I say hello, holding out a flyer for him. "Our first meeting is next week. Think you can make it?"

His eyes darting around to see if anyone is listening, Albert says, "Are you crazy? Why would I want to do that?"

He immediately turns around, leaving me alone with angry thoughts of how I'd like to shake him fiercely, make him take back his sarcastic words. It's been weeks since the incident at the beach and Albert's still in denial. Frustrated, I hurry on to the Chemistry labs where I meet up with

Marsea Grant. Pausing, she says, "Tommy, I heard about the GSA Club. I think it's great—I'll be there."

"Thanks, Marsea," I tell her, as she rushes off to her class.

As I make my way out of the building and head for my car, I think about Marsea's words of support. Maya was right. There are some good people at Roosevelt, and Marsea's one of them. I remember how she stood up for Ankiza that year when someone made a racist comment. At the school assembly, Marsea let the entire student body know that she was Jewish American, reminding students that Jewish Americans also faced discrimination in the United States. Yeah, screw Albert. GSA doesn't need him.

At the Rialto, I try to erase Albert from my thoughts as I prepare for tonight's movies. We're short-handed, so I end up doing everything from running the popcorn machine to collecting tickets at the door. When I finally take my break I catch parts of the movie. It's an intense love story set during World War II, only I don't get to see the ending.

When I get home, Mom is half-asleep on the couch. I tap her lightly on the shoulder to let her know I'm home. Opening her droopy eyelids, Mom straightens out her shoulders, saying, "*Hijo*, I was dreaming about your *abuelita*. We were somewhere shopping together."

"That's nice," I say, turning toward the stairway.

Mom's words force me to pause. "Tomás, I saw the flyer in your room about the new club."

"Oh, yeah?" I say, turning around to look at her.

"It's a good thing what you're doing."

"I know, but someone's already going around trashing our announcements, and then today I tried to invite a friend to the first meeting, and he was rude and obnoxious."

"*Hijo*, don't give up. Stand up for what you believe, no matter what—even your dad would agree with me."

Grimacing, I watch Mom rise slowly from the couch. "You must be kidding, right?"

"Your dad loves you and he only wants the best for you. If you could see him—he goes around bragging to all his *compadres* about how his son is going to be the first one in the family to go to college."

"He does?" Now I'm completely stunned by Mom's startling revelation.

"Yes, *hijo,* so I know he would want you to stand up for what you believe."

Every inch of me wants to believe that Dad understands who I am, only I'm filled with doubts, so I don't say anything. Instead, I tell Mom goodnight, then head upstairs to my room. That night, I lie awake in bed for the longest time thinking about what Mom said. Why can't Dad tell *me* instead of his idiot *compadres* that he's proud of me? Can't Dad see how his silence hurts me?

✳ ✳ ✳

On Tuesday, Jean and I join Mr. Miller in the Art room where our first GSA meeting is going to be held. While we anxiously await to see who will show up, Mr. Miller reminds us that we need to stick closely to our agenda since we only have thirty minutes. He then adds, "I received a call from my friend, Mike Sims, who teaches third grade at

César Chávez Elementary. They're looking for volunteer math tutors to help some of their students who are from México."

"Don't look at me, Mr. Miller," Jean protests. "I'm barely passing Algebra."

"How about you, Tommy?"

"Maybe," I answer, thinking back to all the times I've helped Amanda with her math homework. Mom says I'm patient, but sometimes Amanda's attitude makes me want to slap her.

"Mike said even one hour a week would help."

"I'll find out if I can fit it in with Work Experience," I finally agree.

Mr. Miller thanks me as Maya, Ankiza and Juanita enter the classroom. "Told you we'd be here," Maya triumphantly states. Ankiza and Juanita, who are like Maya's foot soldiers, happily agree with her.

"You're just in time," Mr. Miller says, before they can take a seat, instructing them to arrange the desks in a half-circle.

Marsea Grant is the next one to arrive. She introduces her two friends, Ricki and Kayleigh, whom I recognize from Chemistry last year. I smile at Tim Zimmerman when he arrives with another student that I vaguely recognize from campus. I think back to all the times I've heard male students using Tim as the butt of their homophobic jokes. I'm really glad he's here.

When Mr. Miller signals me that it's time to start, I glance nervously at Jean and she gives me an encouraging nod. After I introduce myself, I say, "My friend, Jean Ornelas, and I came up with the idea to start the first

Gay/Straight Alliance at Roosevelt. I'm sure you all know Mr. Miller—he's going to serve as our advisor."

Now Mr. Miller addresses the group. "Thank you all for coming and I'm thrilled to be your advisor. First, I'd like to say something about our club mission. The mission of the newly formed GSA is not to promote homosexuality or any agenda, but to ensure that all students have equal access to a safe education regardless of their sexual orientation. Our club mission is not to attack anyone or to be divisive, but rather to work toward constructive goals of safety and equality. Having said that, why don't we go around the circle and introduce ourselves. Feel free to share anything you want about why you joined the club."

Jean, who's known for being outspoken and direct, is the first one to talk. "I was really happy when Tommy approached me about forming the GSA. You all know me. I don't much care what other people think or say about me, but I am sick and tired of all the homophobes at Roosevelt. It's about time we did something to change that."

Nodding profusely, Maya introduces herself, then she states, "I'm also excited about Tomas' club. I'm here to offer all my solidarity and support."

"Me too," Ankiza adds, but before she can say anything else, Juanita interrupts.

"I'm Juanita, Tommy's friend, and I also want to help in any way I can with the club."

When Juanita gives me one of her classic dimpled smiles, I suddenly realize this is a moment I won't ever forget. Not just because it's my senior year, but because of the true friends I've made here at Roosevelt. Friends who have stuck by me all these years.

Marsea's soft, poetic voice interrupts my nostalgic thoughts. "Most of you already know who I am from my work with student government on our campus. I want to reiterate my full support for the Gay Straight Alliance." Marsea then turns to look at her two friends, who shyly introduce themselves as Ricki and Kayleigh. The room grows silent as we wait for them to say something more, only they don't.

Tim Zimmerman breaks the silence with his clear, polished voice. "Almost every campus I know of has a Gay Straight Alliance Club—it's about time we follow suit."

Monte Parish is the last one to introduce himself. Now I remember where I've seen him. He's always hanging out with the Christian group on campus. I never thought I'd see someone like him here.

Monte is about to explain why he's interested in being a member of GSA when the bell rings. "Sorry, Monte," Mr. Miller apologizes. "Looks like we're out of time. For our next meeting, why don't each of you bring some ideas for club activities. We'll also need to elect some officers."

"¡Órale!" Jean shouts out, as the meeting comes to an end. We all leave with a smile.

EIGHT

Two days later, I'm going into my U.S. Government class when a voice behind me asks, "How did the fag meeting go?" I hear laughter as I spin around to face Jim Reese, who is with one of his idiot friends.

"That's none of your damn business," I answer, wishing I could smash Jim's face to the ground, but he backs off, mumbling something that I can't make out to his friend.

Hurrying to my assigned seat, I notice that someone has scribbled the word "Fag" in bright red letters on my desk. Disgusted, I rub it off, wondering if Jim put one of his cowardly friends up to this. I wouldn't put it past him. It's a good thing he's on the other side of the classroom or I'd really let him have it.

I take a deep breath, focusing my attention on Mrs. Freberg, who is discussing the United States Bill of Rights and the First Amendment. It gets real interesting when Jackie, who is a student reporter for the school newspaper, raises her hand to ask, "Do First Amendment rights extend to school newspapers?"

Marsea Grant, who is in the front row, instantly replies, "I'm almost certain school administrations can't censor any articles or letters students wish to print."

Nodding, Mrs. Freberg states, "Student press is indeed protected by First Amendment rights, which specifically stipulate freedom of the press. Nonetheless, this has been a controversial topic at schools, universities and colleges throughout the country, where questions have been raised about how much freedom school newspapers should have."

Another student quickly interrupts, "Has anyone actually tried to censor a high school newspaper?"

"As a matter of fact, they have. It's even gone to the Supreme Court. For example, the *Hazelwood School District v. Kuhlmeier* case in 1988, but a more recent example regarding censorship by schools was the 2004 *Dean vs. Utica Community Schools* case. Why don't we turn to page 120 and read the summary of this case?"

A few students groan, while Jim Reese loudly exclaims, "That's so gay."

Jim's homophobic comment generates a few snickers and I wait for Mrs. Freberg to say something, only she acts as if she hasn't heard. Typical, I think to myself, doing my best to remain calm as Mrs. Freberg calls on Jackie to read out loud.

When the period finally comes to an end, I'm eager as hell to get as far away as I can from this stupid class, but Marsea catches up to me at the door. "This is the kind of stuff that we need to put a stop to—teachers like Mrs. Freberg who don't say anything when someone makes a derogatory remark."

"Yeah, I know. It's disgusting."

"GSA needs to address issues like this. We need sensitivity training for teachers like Mrs. Freberg. Roosevelt needs to modify its anti-discrimination policy to include sexual orientation."

"You're damn right," I agree. "I'll mention it to Mr. Miller. Maybe we can put it on the agenda for our next meeting. Thanks, Marsea."

As I hurry down the hallway to CAD class, I realize that it's great to have a student government leader like Marsea in GSA. Marsea is fearless, and if anyone knows the school policies, it's her.

＊ ＊ ＊

As soon as I have the approval to include tutoring as part of Work Experience, I drive to César Chávez Elementary School. I'm more excited than nervous about my first day of tutoring. Since I was a young boy, Mom always told me it was important to help others, so I'm eager to finally be able to do this, especially with little kids who are just learning English.

César Chávez Elementary is the new school that was built last year on the north side of Laguna. Following Mr. Miller's instructions, I park in the visitor's parking lot and then make my way to the front entrance. As I go inside, I'm struck by the huge portrait of César Chávez that hangs on the wall. I remember Maya's comments when we heard the school was going to be named after him. "What a miracle they didn't pick another white person—it's about time they named a school after César Chávez."

After I sign in, the friendly receptionist points out the hallway that will take me to Mr. Sims' classroom. Moving through the hallway, I smile at the colorful drawings on the walls with the students' names written in scraggly cursive. They remind me of the pictures Amanda brings home from school. When I finally open the door to Room 124, I glance around at all the noisy little people scattered in small groups throughout the classroom. My eyes take in the new computer and printer next to the teacher's desk. That's cool, I think to myself, remembering how we were lucky to have a DVD player in our classroom. There is a large bulletin board next to the chalkboard which holds the "Star of the Week," a red-haired freckle-faced boy.

A friendly pot-bellied man, who must be Mr. Sims, signals me from a table at the back of the room where he is working with a group of students. As I move closer, I recognize the little houses made of sticks or tulle that makeup a Chumash Indian village. I think back to how much I enjoyed learning about the Chumash when I was in elementary school. As I approach the table, a curly-haired boy blurts out, "Who are you?"

"Tommy, the math tutor," I sheepishly admit, as Mr. Sims reminds his student that it's not polite to ask impertinent questions.

Smiling, I say, "That's okay, I'm used to it—I have two little sisters."

After he introduces himself, Mr. Sims directs me toward a group of desks where two girls and a dark-skinned boy are working on a science project of an erupting volcano. I'm astonished when Mr. Sims begins speaking in badly accented Spanish. "Mario, ez Tommy, veeno por ayudarte con mateymateecas." As Mario stares at me, Mr. Sims explains, "Sorry about my *gringo* pronunciation. Anyway, this is Mario. His family just arrived from Mexico and he only knows a few words of English, but he's a bright young man. We're working on multiplication and he understands it all, but he's having problems with the math-related terms." Pausing, Mr. Sims points to the empty table near the closet, adding, "It would be terrific if you could review some math vocabulary with Mario."

I barely have time to agree as Mr. Sims is pulled away by another student. Holding out my hand to Mario, I introduce myself in Spanish. "My name is Tomás Montoya. You can call me Tommy. My parents aren't from Mexico, but they speak Spanish, too. I'm here to help you with math."

A huge smile spreads across Mario's perfect little face as I instruct him, in the best Spanish I know, to bring his math worksheets to the empty table. Moments later, we begin to review the multiplication table and I realize Mr. Sims is right about Mario knowing his math. It's only the vocabulary he doesn't understand, so I make him repeat the words out loud several times both in English and Spanish as we do the math problems. Next, I make him print the math vocabulary on a sheet of paper so that he can learn to spell the words, then I have Mario read them back to me several more times. When I give him a practice test on the meaning of each of the words, he passes with flying colors. "You're a good teacher," Mario praises me and I thank him, feeling more confident than I've felt the entire day.

When it's time for me to leave, Mario wants to know if I am coming to help him again. The eager look on his face lets me know that I've made a good impression on him and that soon we will be friends. "Of course I will, " I answer, holding out my hand so that Mario can give me a high five.

When I get back to the apartment, I find Dad out in front changing the oil on his car. Lifting his head up from the open hood, he says, "Tomás, a letter came for you. I put it on top of the TV. I think it's from that university."

My heart racing, I hurry inside and grab the letter off the TV. Opening it slowly, I let out a yell as I read the part where I've been accepted into San Francisco State University. "Is that the letter you've been waiting for?" Mom asks, coming out of the kitchen.

Waving the letter in the air, I exclaim, "Mom, I made it! I'm going to San Francisco State!"

"*Hijo*, I'm so proud of you," she says, hugging me.

Just then, Dad appears in the room. "Was it good news?"

Mom nods, happily explaining that I've been accepted to San Francisco State. I almost faint when Dad states, "*Qué bueno*, Tomás. I knew you'd get in." Dad then goes back outside, leaving me in total disbelief.

With tears in her eyes, Mom whispers, "I told you, *hijo*. Your dad *is* proud of you."

NINE
Ms. Martínez

All week long, I couldn't get thoughts of Andy out of my head, so I decided it would be best to take a trip to Delano and talk to Mom in person about my suspicions. That Thursday evening, while we were having dinner, I told Frank about my plans, asking him if he could accompany me. Frank carefully explained, "Wish I could go, hon, but I have to go into the office this weekend."

Disappointed, I asked, "Isn't there less to do now that tax season has ended?"

"Yes, but I've got several clients the IRS is after and I need to stay on top of that, but please go ahead with your plans. I know how important this is to you."

As I watched Frank refill his wine glass, I knew that it had to be urgent for him to want to stay behind. Frank loved visiting with Mom and Dad. "I don't know how Mom will take it, not having you there to spoil with her cooking."

"Tell your Mom and Dad I had a lot of work—that I'll see them next time."

Frank's curt response made me wonder if he was really sorry he couldn't go with me. Then again, maybe he needed some time alone. It was selfish of me to want to spend every single weekend together.

On Saturday morning, it was almost ten o'clock by the time I was on the road to Delano. As I turned on to highway 46, I thought about my decision not to let Mom and Dad know in advance that I was visiting. It was the only way to avoid Mom's interrogation about the sudden trip. I didn't want to blurt out something I might later regret. Besides, I couldn't imagine raising the subject of Andy's sexuality on the phone.

Driving through the San Joaquin Valley was disturbing and painful. Gazing at the orchards, I thought back to the smell of pesticides that used to fill the air when I was a child. If it hadn't been for César Chávez and Dolores Huerta, the humble people who picked our crops would still be enduring pesticide poisoning, as well as living in run-down migrant shacks. Also, there were all those California prisons. How many men of color continued to fill the state prisons? Sonia once told me that the California State Prison system had the best recruitment and retention program for Chicanos and African Americans. I couldn't help but agree with her, gazing at the state prison that had been built outside of Wasco.

As I approached the outskirts of Delano, I recognized the familiar guard tower and barbed wire fence that bordered their new state prison. Disgusted, I continued on past the new subdivisions that were filling up the open spaces. Nearing the city limits, I pulled onto Main Street. I instantly recognized the familiar businesses as well as the new bank on the corner next to a Starbuck's that hadn't been there before. There was a huge sign on a vacant building that read, *Lofts for Sale.* It was disheartening that even here in Delano, the urbanites were arriving. It wouldn't be long before they forced the Raza out and gentrified the whole area as they were doing in East Los Angeles.

Turning into our old barrio, I was confronted by the beauty of its simplicity. Many off the small wooden-frame houses had beautiful rose bushes in front, which reflected the pride of their homeowners despite their low-economic status. Don Nacho and Doña Aurora's front yard was stunning with the large Virgin of Guadalupe statue. It was surrounded by colorful rosebushes and a variety of statues of Catholic saints that kept growing over the years.

On Adriano Street, I drove slowly past Don Anselmo's house and parked in front of the familiar yellow and pink house that belonged to my parents. Dad, who was outside mowing the lawn, gazed up at me with surprise as I climbed out of the car. I heard him call out, *"Vieja, ven,"* and moments later, Mom appeared at the screen door.

"Working hard?" I asked Dad, opening the wooden gate and moving closer to embrace him.

Pausing to wipe the sweat from his brow, Dad answered, "It's good to see you, *hija.*"

By now, Mom was at my side and after we exchanged a brief hug, she asked, "Is something wrong? You didn't call to tell us you were coming. Where's Frank?"

Explaining that Frank had to work, I hastily added, "I was missing Dad—wanted to find out how his AA meetings are going." Mom was still eyeing me suspiciously, only I avoided her stare. "How's Don Anselmo?" I asked Dad. Don Anselmo had been our neighbor since my parents had first bought the house. When Andy and I were little, Don Anselmo would hire us to cut weeds for him. At first, we were afraid of him, but then we realized Don Anselmo was just a kind man. After his wife died, my parents took it upon themselves to keep an eye on him, as if he were a member of the family.

"*Corajudo*, but he's fine," Dad smiled. "He's with his daughter in Sacramento this week. She practically had to tie him up to get him to go. I'll get your suitcase."

I followed Mom inside, glancing nostalgically at the small living room. It always felt bittersweet returning home. Nothing seemed to change—the same old couch covered with Mom's brown and orange afghan, Dad's familiar recliner in the same spot where he sat every evening watching old reruns of *Gilligan's Island* and *Three's Company*, the neatly arranged photographs on the walls, reminding me that Andy was gone. Yet, I could still feel his presence. I imagined us sitting at the kitchen table playing Monopoly, the colorful arguments each time I caught him cheating. Breathing in deeply, I realized how hard it really was being here.

After I unpacked, I dialed Frank's cell phone, only he didn't answer so I left a brief message letting him know I had arrived. I then went into the kitchen to eat the sandwich Mom had prepared for me. "Where's Dad?"

"He went over to his *compadre*'s. He said to tell you he'd be right back."

There was calmness in Mom's voice. Maybe now was the best time to approach her. She always seemed more relaxed in the kitchen. "Mom," I cautiously began. "You were right to wonder if there was a reason why I made this sudden trip."

Now I had Mom's full attention as she turned away from the sink, drying her hands hastily on her apron. "Mom, was Andy gay?"

Her face turned ashen. "Sandra, *¿estás loca?*" She began to scrub the kitchen sink. I felt my heart thundering as I rose from the table and moved closer to her side, insisting, "Mom, I'm dead serious. That's why I came. I need to know the truth once and for all."

Mom whisked around to face me, her face contorted with anger. "I don't know where you got that crazy idea and you better not say anything about this to your dad." Suddenly, she was gone from the room, her angry words floating in the air. Though I felt guilty for hurting Mom, I'd seen the stark truth in her eyes. It was clear that she'd known Andy was gay and that she'd kept it hidden all these years. Still, I needed to be certain, and for that, there was still one more person I had to see.

TEN
Ms. Martínez

It only took a few phone calls before I was able to locate Andy's best friend, Tony Rivera. After graduating from high school, Tony had attended a local junior college, completing his teaching degree at Cal State Bakersfield. Through Mom's *comadre* grapevine, I knew Tony was now married with two daughters and that he taught history at Delano Middle School. Tony was surprised to hear my voice on the other end of the line. We spent the first five minutes catching up on each other's lives. I talked about Frank and my career as a psychologist. When I questioned Tony about teaching, he proudly confessed, "I always wanted to come back to the barrio and help our kids."

"We could certainly use more people like you, given the high dropout rate in the Latino community," I complimented him. Then, drawing in a deep breath, I continued, "Tony, I was wondering if we could meet today. I need to talk with you about Andy."

There was a slight pause while Tony contemplated my request. I knew he had detected the urgency in my voice. "Sure," he finally agreed. "Today would be good since my wife took my youngest daughter shopping for a prom gown. They'll be gone for hours."

I thanked Tony and before we hung up, I carefully jotted down his address.

Half an hour later, I drove into Almond Valley Estates, one of the new sub-divisions outside of Delano. I couldn't help but admire the modern two- and three-story homes with their pristine landscaping. Following Tony's instructions, I turned left at the small neighborhood park, continuing up Descanso Street until I spotted the old green Volvo Tony had described parked in his driveway. As I descended from the car, Tony walked out the front door. Although he was slightly heavier, I recognized Tony immediately. His hair was shorter, almost like a crew-cut and I spotted a patch of grey at his temples. "Sandy, you look great," Tony said, embracing me. "I'm a little *panzón*," he chuckled, patting his Dallas Cowboy T-shirt.

"What a beautiful neighborhood."

"Yeah, it's a long way from the barrio," he smiled, inviting me inside.

As I sunk into the comfortable beige leather couch, Tony went into the kitchen for refreshments. Gazing around the room, my eyes rested on the fireplace mantle that was lined with family photographs. I felt a tug at my heart. All these years and I was still childless. If only I hadn't lost the baby. My sadness was interrupted by Tony as he returned, handing me a tall glass of iced tea. "You can get dehydrated in this heat if you don't drink enough liquids."

"I'd almost forgotten how hot it gets out here," I said, taking a long drink. Then, breathing in slowly, I began. "Thanks for seeing me Tony. I might as well explain the reason for my visit. This might seem totally out of left field, but I was wondering if you knew if Andy had a secret he was keeping from everyone?"

"What do you mean?" Tony asked, his eyes narrowing.

"What I mean is—was Andy gay? Is that why he took his life?"

Tony shuffled his feet uncomfortably, turning to gaze out the bay window as silence filtered into the room. I waited until he finally looked at me again. "Yes, Andy was gay."

"I thought so," I whispered, feeling as if I were no longer swimming against the current. Lifting my head, I continued, "Why didn't Andy tell me? I thought he trusted me."

Tony leaned forward, his voice hoarse. "You don't know how badly Andy wanted to tell you, it's just that he was afraid he'd disappoint you."

"How could he even think that?"

"I know, Sandy, but you have to understand, he was afraid of being rejected."

"Is that why he killed himself?" I felt the tears stinging my eyes.

"I think so," Tony answered, his voice almost a whisper. "All that week at school, he was so depressed. I tried to convince him to talk to somebody, to your mom, but he kept saying how your mom would hate him, that she was a Catholic and Catholics believed all homosexuals would die in hell."

"But what about me? I never thought that way. Why didn't Andy trust me? I would never have rejected him. I loved him more than anything."

"I know you did, Sandy, and Andy knew it too, but you were away at college. I never thought Andy would take his own life. When he said it that afternoon, I didn't take him seriously. If only I'd told somebody, anybody, then maybe Andy would still be alive. I've had to live with the guilt all these years."

His eyes filled with despair, Tony bowed his head. I found myself wishing I could comfort him, make the guilt disappear. "It's not your fault, Tony. It's not anybody's fault. I'm sorry for bringing up old wounds, but I had to know the truth. That's why I came."

"Have you talked with your Mom about this?" Tony asked, looking up at me with blurry eyes.

"I tried yesterday, but all she did was get angry and deny it. There's no doubt in my mind now that she knew all along that Andy was gay, but she's still not ready to face the truth."

We were silent for a very long moment, then Tony said, "Sandy, you need to know that Andy was very proud of you. He was always bragging about his big sister who was studying at the university."

Blinking back the tears, I whispered, "Thanks Tony. That means a lot to me."

✳ ✳ ✳

Dad was watching the five o'clock news when I walked into the living room. "*¿Dónde andabas?*" he asked, glancing my way.

Although I didn't approve of little white lies, I knew that often times they were unavoidable. "I went for a drive," I replied. "The downtown area sure has grown."

"*Así es*, a lot of new businesses forcing the old ones out."

Just then, Mom appeared in the kitchen doorway, announcing that dinner was ready. I couldn't help but notice that her eyes were red and puffy. Hurrying to the bathroom to wash my hands, I had a sudden flashback to the evening Tommy's mother had shown up at the house with the same puffy red eyes and a desperate look on her face. That night, I had given Mrs. Montoya a pamphlet on PFLAG, informing her that parents of gay and lesbian teens went through their own coming out process. By the end of our visit, Mrs. Montoya had left feeling more hopeful. If only Mom would allow me to help her in that same way.

Dinner seemed long and uncomfortable. Mom barely spoke while Dad rambled on about the new UFO book he was reading. When I asked him about his AA meetings, he said, "I never thought I'd like going there. You know how I hate talking in front of people, but the other night, I finally did and it wasn't so bad."

Hoping to engage Mom in the conversation, I turned to her, asking, "How about you, Mom? Are you still going to the Al-Anon meetings?"

Mom abruptly rose from the table, moving toward the sink. "I go every now and then with one of my *comadres*." Her curt reply let me know she was still hurt. When I offered to wash the dishes, Mom adamantly refused my help.

Back in the living room, Dad said, "Your Mom seems upset—*¿se pelearon otra vez?*"

"No, Dad. We're fine," I lied once more, as Dad focused his attention on an old rerun of *Gilligan's Island*. Reaching for my phone, I dialed Frank, but his voice message came on. How odd, I thought to myself. It was almost ten o'clock and Frank still wasn't home.

Before falling asleep that night, I repacked my suitcase. I was determined to make an early exit before Mom got out of bed. As much as I had hoped to talk with her about Andy, I knew now was not the time. I needed to give Mom some time to process everything. It was best to go home and wait.

ELEVEN
Tommy

I am about to back my Honda out of the school parking lot when my cell phone rings. "Hey, Tommy, it's me— Albert. Can you come over?"

Momentarily stunned by the unexpected call, I ask, "Where are you?"

"At my house—I really need to talk to you."

The urgency in Albert's voice alerts me that something has happened. "I'm on my way to work."

"Please come—I need to talk to someone."

Hesitating, I wonder what could've happened to make Albert contact me. It's been weeks since I gave him my phone number that day at the hospital. When Albert pleads with me again, I finally agree, asking him for his address.

Next, I call Rick, the manager, at the Rialto. I make up a story about having to pick up my little sister at school, that she's sick and there's no one to watch her at home. Rick gets hysterical, repeating how Tuesday is bargain night and it's one of our busiest nights. He finally chills out when I suggest that he call Josh, who has the day off. As we hang up, I can tell he's still not pleased by my sudden absence.

It turns out that Albert lives at the Country Club Estates, which are on the south side of Laguna. Although I've never been to the Country Club before, I know that Ankiza's ex-boyfriend, Hunter, lives there. I never imagined a Latino family living at the Country Club, since it's made up of mostly rich white families. Most people think we're only the gardeners or the cooks. That's why I really want to go to San Francisco State and get a degree. Break all the damn stereotypes.

As I pull up to the gated entry, the watchman asks for my name. After he checks me off his list, he gives me instructions on how to get to Manzanita Court. I circle the golf course until I find Albert's home, which almost takes up an entire block. I thought Maya's house was fancy, but this one looks like a Spanish hacienda with its red-tile roof and lushly landscaped front courtyard. Parking the car, I enter through the wrought-iron gates, admiring the large fountain and terraced garden.

The moment I ring the doorbell, Albert appears in the arched doorway. There are dark circles under his eyes and he seems edgy. "Thanks for coming," he says, motioning for me to go inside. As I follow him through the hallway, I catch a glimpse of a huge swimming pool in the backyard, surrounded by rosebushes and fruit trees. We go into a room which appears to be the den. The walls are lined with bookshelves and there is a fireplace in the corner. "Have a seat," Albert says, reaching for the remote to shut off the small flat screen TV. Gazing around the room, my eyes rest on a large oil painting of a pristine sailboat perched on ocean waves. "That's a scene from the Catalina Islands— Dad likes to sail."

"Oh, yeah," I say, realizing I've never once been on a boat, let alone on an island.

"My parents found out," Albert suddenly blurts out. Turning to gaze into his deep-set eyes, I wait for him to continue. "They were waiting for me when I walked in the door last night. Mom found a letter in my room that I had written to this guy in Tracy. She was hysterical, Dad too. They both screamed at me, then all they did was argue about it. Mom blamed Dad, saying it was his fault, that running the company had always been more important than his son, and that he was never home. Dad started accusing Mom of caring more about shopping and spending money. That's when I couldn't take it any longer, so I locked myself in my room. Only they came after me, pounding on the door like crazy, but I refused to open it. Mom insisted she was calling her therapist tomorrow, that I needed psychological help." Albert pauses, his face flushed with anger. "I can't stand them," he finally continues. "I hate them both."

In an instant, I'm taken back to that awful night when my parents found out the truth. I can still hear Dad's ugly words, "*¡Desgraciado!* I won't have *a joto* in my house." I'd gone to stay at Maya's that night and for the longest time I hated Dad. Not my mom, she always stood by me.

Trying to console Albert, I tell him, "I know this hurts like hell, but at least it's out in the open now."

"How did your parents find out?"

"It's a long story, but it was one of the worst moments of my life."

"Nothing could be worse than last night," Albert whispers.

"Oh, yeah? How about trying to kill yourself."

Shocked by my sudden confession, Albert jerks his head up. Our eyes meet and I feel as if he is about to drown and only I can save him. Inhaling slowly, I recount the entire day leading up to my suicide attempt. I describe the days that followed and how I ended up going from the hospital to Maya's house.

When I'm finished, Albert says, "Maybe that's what I should do—kill myself."

"That's not the answer, Albert."

"Then what am I supposed to do? Pretend everything is okay?"

Shaking my head, I say, "Try to talk to your parents. Be honest with them. If it hadn't been for my mom, I don't know how I would've done it. What about your older sister? Can you talk to her?"

"No, she's too busy at college. As for my parents, all they care about is themselves. Mom's a shopaholic and if Dad's not at the office, he's golfing. My parents don't give a damn about my feelings." Albert's voice is hoarse and he bows his head to hide the tears.

"I thought my parents didn't care about me either. But I found out that it was just as hard for them to accept that I was gay, that they had to go through their own coming out. Now my Dad finally treats me like a human being."

There is a moment of silence, then Albert mutters, "I don't know what I'm going to do—I know Mom's going to insist I see a shrink. Knowing Dad, if I don't do what they say, he'll cut off my allowance and take my credit cards away. Who knows? Maybe it's best to pretend, go along with their sick farce."

"Why don't you come to our next GSA meeting? It's this Thursday. You know our advisor, Mr. Miller." I'm suddenly acutely aware of the importance of our club. Maybe if there had been a Gay Straight Alliance Club at Roosevelt back then, I wouldn't have tried to take my life.

"You've gotta be kidding?" Albert snickers.

"What would be so wrong with that?"

"Then for sure everyone at school would know I'm gay. It's bad enough they've all been gossiping about me. No, I couldn't do that."

I feel like grabbing Albert by the shoulders and shaking the denial out of him. Can't he see that if anyone understands his fear of rejection, it's me? My face burning, I lean forward. "Listen to me, Albert. I used to be ashamed of who I was. I felt dirty and ugly inside until I came out. Now I'm finally free and I'm proud to be who I really am. No more lies, no more pretending, that's what it's all about, Albert. It's about what you think of yourself, not what others think."

"I'm sorry, but I can't. I can't go to that meeting."

Although I'm disappointed by Albert's reaction, I remember how Ms. Martínez said I can't make him come out, that Albert has to want to do it himself.

"Listen, you better go. Mom's due any moment. She thinks I went to school today, so I have to pretend I just got home."

"Okay, but think about what I said. The club meeting is on Thursday."

"Thanks, but no thanks," Albert repeats, as I stand up to leave.

TWELVE
Tommy

While Mr. Miller welcomes everyone back, I glance around the room, taking in the same group of students who were at our first GSA meeting. Albert is the only person missing. I thought he might come after we talked on Tuesday, but I guess I was wrong. Still, I'm glad everyone has returned except for Ankiza, who had to attend a Senior Class meeting since she's one of the officers this year. Rina is the only new person today. Yesterday, she stopped me in the hallway to explain why she was coming, "I have an uncle in Puerto Rico who's gay and Mom says the family's always been in total denial."

Welcoming the club members back, Mr. Miller explains, "Now that we're an official club, we need to elect officers."

Jean is exuberant. "I think Tommy should be the President since it was his idea to start the club. And if it's okay with everyone, I'd love to serve as VP."

"Thanks," I tell Jean, feeling proud as everyone unanimously agrees with Jean's nominations.

When Mr. Miller announces that we will need a secretary, as well as a student representative for the inter-club council, Marsea eagerly raises her hand. "I'd like to be the student rep since I've served on the school council before." She turns to her friend, Ricki, asking, "Would you like to serve as secretary?"

Happily surprised, Ricki says, "That would be fun."

By now, Mr. Miller has written the tentative names of the officers on the board so that we can vote. We take a few minutes to write our votes on scraps of paper, then we wait patiently while Mr. Miller tallies them. After a few minutes, he clears his voice and announces, "Congratulations to Tommy, the new President of GSA and to his Vice President, Jean Ornelas. Our club secretary is Ricki Sharpe and the student representative is Marsea Grant."

Rina gives me a hefty slap on the back as Mr. Miller turns the meeting over to me. With my voice uneven, I thank everyone for their support. I firmly state, "One of the first issues on our agenda as a club should be to modify Roosevelt's anti-discrimination policy."

Nodding fiercely, Marsea says, "I know for a fact that the school district code only discusses discrimination based on race, gender and ethnicity. It says nothing about sexual orientation."

"I believe you're right about that," Mr. Miller agrees.

"Then we absolutely need to change that," Maya concludes, sounding just like her mom, the professor.

"How do we go about doing that?" Tim Zimmerman asks.

We fix our gaze on Mr. Miller, waiting for his response. "First we need to get a copy of the school district conduct code and then we need to meet with the principal to discuss what GSA is proposing. Mr. Marshall can advise us on how to proceed. I'll set up an appointment to speak with him after school today."

Marsea raises her hand to speak again, "I'd also like to see us organize some kind of diversity forum like we had that year when that awful prom incident happened. This would help raise awareness with Roosevelt's teachers. I was disgusted the other day in U.S. Government when Jim Reese used the word gay in a derogatory way in class and Mrs. Freburg didn't even blink an eye."

"That's nothing," Rina offers. "I hear the word faggot almost on a daily basis in class or in the hallways. Sometimes I feel like punching someone out."

"*Lucha libre* here she comes!" Maya says, and we all smile when Rina raises her fist in the air.

Marsea's freshman friend, Kayleigh, boldly admits, "I get the nastiest remarks when someone finds out I have two moms. I can't stand it. Sometimes I stand up to them, but most of the time I go home crying."

Now Monte Parish, who has remained silent until now, offers his own opinion. "I think Marsea's idea about a diversity forum is a good one. Teachers need to be aware of the harassment that goes on at our school toward anyone who is different."

"Yes, a forum would be an effective way to raise awareness," Mr. Miller agrees, "Why don't we put it on the agenda for our next meeting?"

As the bell rings and the meeting comes to an end, Jean turns to give me a high-five. "Congratulations, *Señor Presidente!*"

Maya and Juanita give me their own high fives, while Rina gives me a hardy slap on the back. We quickly file out of the room. Promising to call Maya later, I head for the nearest exit.

Minutes later, I'm in CAD class, admiring the three-dimensional bungalow I've designed. It's almost finished except for the windows. I have a sudden flashback to the windows in Albert's den. I wonder if Albert talked with his parents; if he told them the truth. I had hoped Albert would attend our GSA meeting. *Ni modo*, as Mom often says.

Mr. Giles appears at my side, forcing me away from my thoughts. Praising my design project, he says, "Tommy, with your natural talent for design, I do hope you're planning on studying architecture or graphic design at the university."

"Thanks Mr. Giles. I'm not sure yet what I'd like to major in, but I just received my official acceptance letter from San Francisco State."

"That's no surprise. Congratulations," Mr. Giles compliments me, as the bell goes off.

I'm at my locker when Albert appears at my side. "Hey, Tommy. Do you have a minute?"

"Sure," I answer, flinging my books inside my locker. As I turn around to face him, I'm tempted to ask why he didn't come to the meeting, but I decide it's better to let him bring it up.

"I wanted to let you know that everything's cool again, with my parents I mean." Glancing around to make sure no one is listening to our conversation, Albert continues. "I went with my mom to see a shrink. She thinks it will make me normal. I've agreed to go once a week so that I can keep my parents off my back."

I can see right through Albert's phony words. He's only fooling himself if he thinks that's the answer. When I don't say anything, Albert shrugs, "That's all I wanted to say," then he disappears in the crowded hallway, leaving me disappointed and frustrated as I hurry off to my car.

THIRTEEN

"Have you seen the Rough Rider today?" Jean asks, when I meet up with her near the water fountain. Shaking my head, Jean hands me a copy of the school newspaper. "Can you believe it? After they printed that nice article on GSA, all hell broke loose. Wait until you read all these nasty notes to the editor about our club."

"I'll read them in class," I say, hurrying off to Senior English. While Mrs. Harrison is reviewing on the board the key elements of our next essay, I pull the newspaper out from under my book and begin to read: *I think it's disgusting that a homosexual club has been formed on our campus. Those people are sick and they need help, not a club.*

The next letter is even worse: *The Bible says homosexuality is a sin. In Lev. 18:22, it states: "Thou shalt not lie with mankind as with womankind. It is an abomination." Homosexuality is a sin. Someone is not born a homosexual, but is born in sin. God says continued sin is addictive and is wrong. We don't need a club on our campus to promote this sinfulness. Come join our Christian group and God will help you change your life and find peace.*

Both of the letters are signed, but with no last name. Now I understand why Jean was upset. I'm surprised by the next letter, which is supportive: *We live in a country where everyone is entitled to freedom of thought and speech, so I think anyone who is gay has a right to form a club to express their views.*

My satisfaction is short-lived, for the next letter presents another vicious attack on our club and anyone who is gay. This one really makes me mad. It blatantly states all homosexuals are deviants that need psychiatric help. Once again, the Bible is quoted to support the idea that homosexuality is a sin. The letter ends by stating that clubs like GSA denigrate the Son of God. Crumpling up the newspaper, I focus my attention back on Mrs. Harrison's lecture.

At lunch time, I join Tyrone, Maya and Ankiza at Foster Freeze. As soon as we're seated at a booth with our orders, the conversation turns to the hateful letters. "Man, they're out for blood," Tyrone says.

"That's no surprise to me," Maya states, glancing at Ankiza. "Remember years back when someone left that hateful letter at your locker?"

"I'll never forget that," Ankiza says, reaching for some chili fries. "I guess I naively thought things had improved at Roosevelt."

"Are you kidding?" Maya says with her usual cynicism. "Ever since GSA was formed, all the bigots have banded together, trying to poison everyone with their hatefulness. I can't stand it."

"Hey, Tommy," Tyrone interrupts. "If anyone tries anything, remember Rudy and I've got your back."

Not Rudy, I think to myself. He hasn't come to a single meeting. Oh, well, screw him. Before I can respond to Tyrone, Maya says, "That's all we need, for the Macho

Men to start a fight. Ty, that's not the way to do it and you know it."

Now Tyrone smiles sheepishly. "Yeah, I know, but Jim Reese and some of his buddies could sure use some ass-kicking."

"Maya's right," I finally interject. "It's best to stay calm. Use our brains."

Ankiza pauses from eating her fries to say, "You know, at our meeting last week, Marsea brought up the idea of organizing a forum."

Maya's face suddenly takes on an intense look that reminds me of her Professor Mom. "That's exactly what we need—a forum with speakers. That way, we could address all this anti-gay rhetoric."

"That's my babe," Tyrone says, nibbling on Maya's ear.

"I'll mention it to Jean before our next meeting," I agree, feeling hopeful and more grateful than ever for my supportive friends. Now, if only Rudy could be like that.

✳ ✳ ✳

At Cesar Chávez Elementary School, I know exactly where to find Mario's classroom. As I open the door, I can hear excited kid voices. All of the desks have been rearranged in clusters of three and the students are working on brightly colored piñatas of all shapes and sizes. The moment he spots me, Mario rushes to my side. In Spanish, he insists, "Come see my piñata. Mr. Sims says it's one of the best."

I follow Mario to his desk where two little girls are working on their own piñatas that are shaped like sea animals. They giggle when I say hello to them. Holding up his odd-shaped turquoise-blue piñata, Mario eagerly explains, "It's a guitar. My dad loves to play the guitar."

I compliment Mario on his piñata as Mr. Sims appears at our side. "We're doing a cultural unit on Cinco de Mayo. We go over the history, then we make piñatas."

"That's really nice," I say, thinking to myself how important it is that kids are learning about the historical significance of Cinco de Mayo. When I was in grade school, it was mostly about George Washington and the pilgrims.

As I follow him to his desk for today's math worksheets, Mr. Sims explains, "Mario's stuck on these word problems, but I know it's only because he doesn't know English. Would you please help him translate?"

"Sure thing," I say, instructing Mario to follow me to the same table in the back.

"I got an A on my last multiplication test," Mario proudly confesses as we sit down.

"Terrific," I tell him, focusing my attention on the first word problem: *A new school bought magic markers for all of the classrooms. There are six markers in each package and each box of markers contains 4 packages. How many markers are there in four boxes?*

As soon as I translate the problem in Spanish for Mario, he gives me the correct answer. Next, I ask him to read the problem back to me in English, which he does, but not without struggling with the pronunciation. "Why don't you write some of these words down so that you can practice them at home?" I suggest. I wait until Mario's finished before I move on to the next word problem. This one is about counting plastic straws, only I don't know the Spanish word for straws. When I explain this to Mario, he repeats the word, "popotes." I can tell he's pleased to teach me a word in Spanish. Once again, Mario gives me the correct answer to the word problem. After he reads the problem out loud, I have Mario repeat a few key words and phrases like "How many?" I then have him write out the words in English.

"My mom has straws at home for my baby sister," Mario shares, as he writes the word "straw" in his notebook several times so that he won't forget it. "Do you have a baby sister?" he asks, gazing up at me.

"Are you kidding? I have two. Amanda's the baby, she's nine and María is an eleven-year-old monster."

Mario chuckles, admitting he also has a brother, who is in first grade.

By the time Mr. Sims announces that it's time to go home, Mario and I have completed the last worksheet. Reminding him to practice his list of English words, I say goodbye to Mario. I hurry out of the classroom before I get trampled on by the little people who are racing to put their things away. As I head back down the hallway, I think about how rewarding it is to work with young kids, especially with someone like Mario who looks up to me. All of a sudden, I find myself wondering if maybe I should become a teacher. The thought never entered my mind until today. I always thought I wanted to be an architect or a graphic designer. Now I'm not so sure.

FOURTEEN
Ms. Martínez

Frank was gone by the time I got out of bed, leaving me a note on the kitchen table that he was going into his office to finish up some paperwork. Was it my imagination or was Frank spending more time in his office on weekends? It seemed as if we never went on hikes anymore like we used to on Saturdays. Still, I needed to remember how patient Frank had been with me and my long hours when I first started up my practice.

My cell phone interrupted my thoughts. It was Diego calling from San Francisco to say that Bryan was home from the hospital. "He's feeling better," Diego said, with a long sigh.

"I'm glad to know that. I'll call Frank at the office and let him know."

Surprised, Diego asked, "He's in his office on a Saturday?"

I went into a lengthy explanation of how the end of tax season was still a busy time for Frank. Diego sympathized with Frank for having to sacrifice his weekend. We chatted for a few more minutes about Bryan's new medications. As we hung up, I promised that Frank and I would go visit them as soon as we were able to get away.

After I finished my second cup of espresso, I stepped out to the backyard. As I reached for the hose to water my pathetic-looking plants, I thought about Mom and her beautiful garden. I hadn't talked with her since my visit to Delano. It had never been my intention to hurt Mom, but it was time to let go of the lies, to be honest about Andy's death. Yet, I knew I could not force the truth out of Mom. I needed to heed the same advice I had given Tommy about Albert.

Walking back into the kitchen, I heard the phone ring again and when I answered it, a jubilant Juanita exclaimed, "I have great news, Ms. Martínez! Celia had a baby girl last night!"

"She did? Congratulations! Your parents must be thrilled."

"Yeah, they are—Apá's already planning a big *pachanga* for the baptism!"

Smiling, I asked about the baby's weight and the name Celia had given her. Juanita answered, "I don't remember how much she weighed, but her name is Jade. Apá didn't like it at first, but when Celia told him she was adding Francisca, my grandma's name, he got over it."

"Jade is a beautiful name, very symbolic in Mexican culture."

"I didn't know that, but Amá wanted to make sure I called you. Oh yeah, Celia said to remind you that you and Frank are going to be the *padrinos*!"

"Tell Celia not to worry, that we haven't forgotten."

As we hung up, I felt the familiar wrenching in my heart, wishing it were me giving birth, celebrating Frank's first child. Forcing away the bitter thoughts, I dialed Frank's cell phone and his voice mail came on. I left a brief message, then I went into my office.

I was in the middle of updating my notes on a client, when I suddenly burst into tears. Putting my head down on a pile of papers, I cried softly for the baby I'd lost, flooded with images of the day I'd miscarried. Frank's grief-stricken eyes, his soothing voice, "It's okay, hon. We'll try again."

After several minutes, the tears subsided and I was able to lift my head, hoping to concentrate once again on the file in front of me, only I couldn't. Distraught, I reached for the phone and dialed Sonia's number. Hearing the desperation in my voice, Sonia convinced me to meet her at the small coffeehouse in my neighborhood.

Half an hour later, I was seated with Sonia in the outside patio of Gitano's, listening to the soothing sounds of the water fountain. "Now tell me, *mujer,* what's going on?" Sonia cautiously asked.

With a weary smile, I replied, "Why is it I can't keep anything from you?"

"Because I'm your *comadre,* that's why," Sonia insisted, her brown eyes narrowing.

Gazing at Sonia's calm face, I realized she was right. Over the years, we'd helped each other survive the most difficult battles—Sonia's divorce from Armando, Dad's alcoholism, her mother's battle with Alzheimer's, Brian's battle with HIV. The list went on and on and we were still here, leaning on each other for help and support.

After a very long moment, I gathered the courage to speak. "Juanita called this morning to let me know Celia had a baby girl." My voice breaking, I continued. "I feel happy for Celia, but all the hurt came up and I completely fell apart."

Sonia reached out to caress my hand. "Sandy, those feelings are absolutely normal. It takes a long time to get over any kind of loss. Isn't that what you tell your clients?"

My voice barely a whisper, I nodded. "I know, but I feel so empty inside."

Handing me a Kleenex, Sonia waited while I blew my nose and wiped away the tears, then she said, "Grief comes at the weirdest times. Sometimes, the smallest things trigger a memory of Mom and I find myself crying for her."

We were both silent and I felt the grief Sonia had undergone with her mother's illness. Feeling selfish, I whispered, "I'm sorry, Sonia. I shouldn't be bothering you with this. I know how hard it's been for you this past year."

"Don't be silly. Remember, we're *comadres*. Have you gone to any of the support group meetings anymore?"

"Not for a long time."

"Well, you might think about doing that again."

"I'm fine, really I am. After all, I'm the shrink in case you've forgotten."

At that, we both laughed and the tension in my body began to disappear. "Now tell me, what's that crazy husband of yours up to today?" Sonia asked.

"Frank had to work," I confessed, wishing I could divulge my suspicions about Frank's recent behavior, only I couldn't. Since Glenn had proposed to her, Sonia was excited again about the idea of marriage. Who was I to burst her bubble?

Sonia's eyes danced as she explained that Glenn was at another MEXA car wash. "He invited me along, but I wanted to have breakfast with Maya. Now that she's a graduating senior, we hardly see each other."

"I can't believe Maya and Juanita are seniors," I said, feeling myself relax even more as we began to talk about Maya's graduation plans and their upcoming visit to the Stanford campus.

✳ ✳ ✳

Frank was stretched out on the couch watching a Dodger game when I walked through the front door. "Hi, hon," he greeted me, sounding like the caring husband I knew and loved.

"I tried calling you earlier. Diego called to say Brian's home from the hospital."

"Yes, I know. I spoke with Dad this morning."

"And there's more good news. Celia had her baby— Jade Francisca."

Frank sat up, cheering loudly, then he went into his favorite Marlon Brando godfather impersonation.

"You'll make a terrifying *padrino*," I teased, when he finally ended his dramatic scene.

"How about we celebrate with dinner and a movie? The new vampire comedy is showing downtown. I'll buy the popcorn. You buy the dinner."

FIFTEEN
Ms. Martínez

Mondays were always jam-packed. Clients were non-stop, frantic for advice or simply wanting to unload after an intense weekend. Today's session with Mark had gone very well. It had taken months before I was able to get him to trust me and talk about his feelings. Latino clients were often the hardest to reach, especially the men. In Latino culture, men were perceived as the patriarchal pillars of strength. Talking about their feelings was considered a sign of weakness. Most Latino men were conditioned to believe they weren't "real men" if they disclosed their true emotions.

As I was reflecting on my breakthrough with Mark, the receptionist called to say that a young man by the name of Tommy was waiting in the lobby. I told her to send him right in and seconds later, Tommy walked into my office. "What a nice surprise, " I said, inviting him to take a seat on my couch.

"I was on my way to tutor at César Chávez Elementary and wondered if I could talk to you about something."

"Perfect timing. My next appointment was cancelled. I didn't know you were tutoring."

Tommy's green eyes sparkled like emeralds. "Yeah, I'm helping this kid, Mario, with his math. It's a lot of fun. Mario's from Mexico and he's really smart, but he doesn't speak English."

"Mario's lucky to have you," I said, thinking about all the recent immigrant-bashing. Why was it that immigrants were always blamed for society's problems?

"I've even been thinking it would be cool to be a teacher," Tommy said, interrupting my thoughts. "Maybe get my degree in teaching at San Francisco State."

"Really? That would be nice. California needs more teachers, especially if they're bilingual like you."

Nodding, Tommy gave a dramatic sigh. "Ms. Martínez, I followed your suggestion and my friend, Jean Ornelas, and I formed the first GSA club at Roosevelt. Only last week it got kind of nasty. There were some real hateful letters in our school newspaper about our club. So we were thinking about maybe having some kind of diversity forum at our school. So, I wanted to run this by you, see what you think."

"That's a great idea. As a matter of fact, I know the President of PFLAG. I bet they'd be more than happy to participate. You might also check with Laguna University. They have a strong Gay and Lesbian Student Organization."

"Thanks, Ms. Martínez. I'll do that," Tommy said, rising to his feet. "I have to go or I'll be late for tutoring."

As I closed the door behind him, I felt a sense of pride in the confident young man Tommy had now become.

✳ ✳ ✳

Once I'd seen my final client of the day, I gathered up my briefcase and the gift I'd bought for Celia's baby. I hurried out to my car, wishing Frank had been able to accompany me to the Chavezes. Oh, well, I thought to myself, at least he had called Juanita's family to congratulate them.

The moment I rang the doorbell, Juanita opened the door. "Hi, Ms. Martínez," she smiled, inviting me inside. Markey was close behind, waving his new Batman at me.

"I have Joker, too," he enthusiastically stated.

I patted him on his curly head. "My brother was also a big fan of Batman when he was your age," I said, following Juanita into the small, but familiar living room. Taking a seat on the couch, I asked, "How's Celia feeling?"

"She's acting like a queen if you ask me. Says she can't do anything around the house 'cause it hurts. But the baby's real cute."

Just then, Mrs. Chávez came out of the kitchen with Rosario, who happily exclaimed, "We made *sopapillas!*"

"Mmm—I love *sopapillas,*" I said, standing up to embrace Mrs. Chávez.

"Carlos is working, but I told him you were coming by to see Francisca," Mrs. Chávez explained in her melodic Spanish accent.

Juanita frowned. "We call her Jade."

Amused by her comment, I said, "I understand Mr. Chávez is already planning the baptism."

Mrs. Chávez smiled. "Carlos said to ask you if we could plan the baptism for next month, so we can go talk with Father Mike next week."

"Yes, that would be perfect. Frank won't be as busy as he is now. He said to tell you he was sorry he couldn't come with me today."

Mrs. Chávez gave me a warm smile. "We know how busy he is."

We were interrupted by Celia as she walked into the room with Lupita, who was proudly carrying Jade Francisca. "Don't drop her," she scolded Lupita, turning to give me a big hug as I congratulated her.

"Can I hold her?" I asked, handing Celia the gift I had brought for the baby.

Nodding, she carefully took the baby from Lupita and placed her in my arms. "Her name is Jade Francisca, but Apá's already calling her Panchita."

"She's beautiful," I said, consumed by pangs of sadness mixed with joy. I rocked the baby gently as Celia hastily unwrapped the gift.

"Thanks, Ms. Martínez," Celia said, holding up the cute pink and yellow dress for everyone to see. "It's real cute."

"I'm glad you like it. It's a little big, but I'm certain little Miss Jade Francisca will fit into it quickly."

"It's my turn to hold her," Rosario cried, as I handed the baby back to Celia.

Warning her little sister to be careful, Celia carefully placed Jade Francisca in Lupita's arms.

"She's going to be so spoiled," Juanita admitted. "All we do is hold her."

"I tell them they need to let her cry sometimes," Mrs. Chávez sighed, but Celia and Lupita quickly came to their niece's defense.

"Well at least they'll be plenty of babysitters to go around," I smiled, asking Celia when she would be able to return to school.

"Next week, I hope. Amá said she'll watch the baby while I'm at school and on the days that she can't, I'll take her to the nursery."

Celia had been attending classes at the TAPP Program, which was an academic program at the local continuation high school whose main objective was to help pregnant teens complete their high school degree. "That's a good plan," I agreed, feeling proud of Celia and all the teen girls who became pregnant and refused to give up on their dreams.

When Mrs. Chávez reappeared in the room with coffee and homemade *sopapillas*, I couldn't resist. Half an hour later, I walked out of the apartment with another plate of *sopapillas* for Frank and a sense of excitement about the upcoming baptism.

SIXTEEN
Tommy

I can't believe my eyes when Rudy walks into the room with Juanita and Sheena. I never thought I'd see Rudy at GSA, but I guess I was dead wrong. He really is my friend after all. With a quick glance at the clock, I call the meeting to order. Looking directly at Rudy, I say, "Thanks for coming, everyone. Yesterday Mr. Miller, Jean and I met with the school principal about modifying the school's anti-discrimination code. Mr. Miller, would you like to say something?"

Mr. Miller, who is perched on the edge of his desk, stands up to speak. "I have some encouraging news. Mr. Marshall was very supportive. He agreed that the district code needs to include harassment based on sexual preference. Mr. Marshall is going to meet with the Superintendent of Schools so that they can put this on the agenda for the next school board meeting."

Several students clap, while Rina bellows out a few cheers. That's all Rudy needed to fling a few insults at Rina, who promptly tells him to shut his face. Waiting for them to get quiet, Mr. Miller adds, "I'll continue to keep you updated on this."

Next, Mr. Miller, turns to Jean, who has raised her hand to speak. "At the last meeting it was suggested that we organize a forum to raise awareness about LGBT issues. By now, I'm sure you've all read the hateful letters in the school newspaper, so what do you think?"

"I've been looking online and I've found several high schools that have had similar forums with a diverse group of speakers," Marsea explains.

"Having a forum would be awesome," Tim agrees. "Maybe we could even invite Laguna University's LGBT group to participate.

Glancing at Tim, I confess, "I ran the idea for a forum by Ms. Martínez. She knows someone from PFLAG who might be interested in speaking."

"We absolutely have to include Ms. Martínez on that panel," Maya insists. "She's always been there for us." Juanita enthusiastically seconds the idea, as several students nod in complete agreement.

Ricki, who is frantically trying to record the club minutes on her laptop, interrupts to say, "Slow down, will you? So we're having a forum with the following speakers—Ms. Martinez, someone from PFLAG, someone from LGBT—is that it?"

"What about a parent?" Tim suggests.

"I know my mom would love to be do it," Jean offers.

"Parent participation on the panel would be phenomenal," Mr. Miller agrees.

"Would Tommy and I also be on the panel?" Jean asks, as Mr. Miller shakes his head, explaining that we would be the moderators.

Then Mr. Miller directs his attention back to the group. "All the GSA members should be present that day. Bring along anyone you know that can offer support, because I'm certain the opposing side will be there once they hear about the forum."

"You better believe Roosevelt's Christian Club will be there," Maya frowns.

"That's for sure—they're always trying to convert everyone on campus," Kayleigh admits, while Monte nods in agreement.

Rudy finally offers his opinion. Puffing out his chest, he brags, "Why worry when you've got Rina and me as body-guards?"

Mr. Miller chuckles when Rina yells out "Mosca Patrol!" Then he says, "We most certainly want the Christian Club members to attend. It's important to include different viewpoints so that we're not accused of excluding anyone." Reaching for his BlackBerry, Mr. Miller continues, "We need to pick a date ASAP since the school year is quickly coming to a close. How about the second Friday of May? It should be after school so that parents and faculty can attend."

Tommy is quick to follow. "Let's vote on that date now. All ayes, raise their hand."

Jean's hand is the first one to go up and it's soon followed by everyone in the room.

✳ ✳ ✳

When I arrive at César Chavez Elementary, I'm forced to park across the street since the guest parking lot is completely full. That's no surprise since today is Mario's Cinco de Mayo classroom celebration. Mario was excited that I had agreed to come as his special guest, especially since his mom was bringing food to the party.

Hurrying inside the school building, I make my way to Mario's classroom. When I open the door, I'm greeted by total chaos. None of the students are in their seats and they appear more hyper than usual. There are cut outs of *papel picado* hanging from the ceiling along with a variety of colorful piñatas. I recognize Mario's funny-shaped guitar hidden among them. A long table covered with a variety of dishes has been placed in front of the chalkboard.

The moment he sees me, Mario springs across the room. "Come meet my mom," he hollers.

Mr. Sims, who is talking with a parent, walks over to greet me. He is wearing a bright red and green Mexican vest with a matching green tie. "Glad you could make it. There's plenty of food left. How about something to eat?"

"It really smells good," I nod, only Mario grabs me by the arm and pulls me to the other side of the room. We pause before two mothers who are busy directing the clean-up crew of little people. I'm struck by the contrast between Mrs. Guzmán, who is short and dark-skinned, and the tall blonde and blue-eyed lady standing next to her. I stretch out my hand to Mrs. Guzmán, who thanks me in Spanish for helping Mario with his school work. Gazing into her kind eyes, I can't help but think how much she resembles my grandma who lives in Texas.

As I shake Mrs. Thompson's hand, she bluntly admits, "I wish I could speak Spanish like that. I studied it in high school, but I've forgotten most of it."

"That happens. Sometimes I even forget how to say something and I have to ask my parents."

Mrs. Guzmán, who has been listening politely despite the fact that she doesn't understand English, interrupts to ask me what part of Mexico my parents are from. "Both my parents were born here," I explain, "but my grandparents were originally from Chihuahua."

Mrs. Guzmán's eyes grow even brighter as she proudly admits, "We're from Michoacán."

When Mrs. Thompson asks if I've eaten, Mrs. Guzmán insists I follow her to the food table where she serves me a huge plate of enchiladas. "The rice is already cold," she apologizes, "but the enchiladas are still warm."

"My mom makes the best enchiladas!" Mario brags, as we find a place to sit. Aware that Mario is watching me attentively, I take a huge bite. After a few seconds, I pause to tell him, "These are the best enchiladas I've ever had."

Mario is breathless as he jumps to his feet and races to tell his mom. When he returns, I ask him what else they did to celebrate Cinco de Mayo. "It was so much fun. Mr. Sims played Mariachi music. There was one song, "*Son de la negra,*" that my Mom always plays at home."

"Did your mom recognize it?"

"Yes, she even got up and showed Mr. Sims how we dance to it in Mexico."

"That's real cool," I say, smiling to myself at the thought of Mrs. Sims trying to dance with Mario's mom.

"We also saw a play—it had Benito Juárez and the Battle of Puebla. "

"It sounds like you learned a lot about the history of Cinco de Mayo?"

"Me, I already knew most of it," Mario brags, "but the other kids didn't."

Just then, Mrs. Guzmán reappears at my side. "I wanted to thank you again for helping Mario with math. His father and I didn't get much schooling in Mexico, so it's hard for us to help him. "

Mario suddenly interrupts to tell me about yesterday's math test and how he only missed two problems. "Mr. Sims said I got the highest grade in the class."

"And it's all because of your help," Mrs. Guzmán quickly adds.

"*De nada*," I proudly say, feeling as if I've just won an NBA championship.

SEVENTEEN

Mr. Miller and Jean are in the auditorium, setting up the table and chairs for the speakers, when I arrive with Juanita, Maya and Tyrone. "How can we help?" I ask, and Mr. Miller points to the microphones on the floor.

"We need to set one up at each end of the bleachers. They're for the audience to use for Q and A."

With Maya and Juanita's help, Tyrone takes the two microphones over to the bleachers where they find the perfect spot for them. "I sure hope we get a good crowd," I tell Jean, who gives me a reassuring nod. Just then, Marsea walks into the gym with Ricki and Kayleigh. When they join us, Mr. Miller lets them know he's reserved the first row for our club members.

As Ricki and Kayleigh head for the bleachers, Marsea admits, "I personally invited the student council members."

Maya, who has just rejoined the group with Juanita and Tyrone at her side, says, "I doubt that they'll come. They're too conservative."

When Monte and Tim walk up to join us, Mr. Miller announces, "Good—all our GSA members are here."

All of a sudden, Jean starts to wave her hands in the air at the tall bulky woman entering the gym. "Over here, Mom," she shouts, as Mrs. Ornelas heads in our direction and comes to a halt next to her daughter. After she introduces her to Mr. Miller, Jean introduces her mom to the entire group assembled around her. It's hard to contain my excitement at meeting a parent like Mrs. Ornelas, who accepted Jean was gay from the moment she found out. It doesn't seem possible, but it's true. Lucky Jean, I think to myself.

We're interrupted by Ms. Martínez, who promptly arrives with Janet Finch, the President of PFLAG. Mr. Miller is introducing himself when, Lance Young, the president of Laguna University's LGBT walks through the door. Once all of the introductions have been made, Mr. Miller describes the format for the evening, indicating that Jean and I will be the moderators.

As we take our assigned seats, I fix my gaze on the groups of people that are filing into the auditorium. The first person I spot is Rina, who is walking in with Ankiza and her dad. My stomach tightens when I recognize several teachers seated in the front bleachers with some parents. "Looks like a good turnout," I whisper nervously to Jean, still hoping to find Albert among the crowd.

At exactly seven o'clock, Mr. Miller approaches the podium and introduces himself as the advisor to GSA. He then gives a brief history of our club, emphasizing GSA's objective is to ensure that there is no discrimination at Roosevelt based on sexual orientation. Mr. Miller concludes with a strong direct statement. "Let me reiterate, we are not here to promote a gay lifestyle or to say gays are better. Our hope, with this diversity forum, is to begin a respectful dialogue."

Next, Mr. Miller introduces me as the President of GSA. I can hear a few cheers as I approach the podium and begin to explain in a high, uneven voice, "Each speaker on our panel will have approximately five minutes to speak. When each of the panelists have finished, we will open it up for questions or comments from the audience. Our first speaker this evening is Janet Finch, the President of Laguna's local chapter of PFLAG."

Thanking GSA for inviting her to be on the panel, Mrs. Finch says, "I'm honored to have served as the President of PFLAG for the past two years. For those of you who may not know, PFLAG is an acronym for Parents and Families of Lesbians and Gays. I first became a member of PFLAG when I found out my son, Chad, was gay. I wanted to learn how to accept the fact that my son was gay and to find out what his life would be like. Chad was in junior high when my husband and I first found out he was gay. My husband had the hardest time with this. He wanted to kick Chad out of the house, but I wouldn't let him. I guess I always knew deep down inside that Chad was gay. He was always harassed in school, but I was in denial about everything. It has taken me a long time to educate myself and to understand that being gay is not a choice, and that Chad is the same son I've always loved, that he did nothing wrong. "

There are several loud claps as Mrs. Finch continues. "PFLAG is a tremendous support system for parents, who go through their own coming out process. As parents of someone who is gay or lesbian, we often feel guilty and blame ourselves. PFLAG helps parents understand that we did nothing wrong, that we need to love and support our children, let them know they are fine just as they are. I certainly don't know what I would have done without the support of PFLAG. PFLAG is also instrumental in educating teachers. We provide workshops for teachers, staff and administrators on how to deal with harassment when it is directed at someone who is gay or lesbian. We also provide information on how to implement Safe School policies. The only way we can get past fear and hatred is through education. You can't make anyone gay that is not already gay. That's why education and raising awareness are so important." Glancing at her watch, Mrs. Finch thanks the audience, saying, "I've brought some brochures on PFLAG and we also have a website for anyone that is interested."

Approaching the podium, Jean waits for the applause to subside before she introduces herself as the Vice President of GSA. Then she candidly admits, "This is a first. Now I get to introduce my mom, Pat Ornelas." With a huge grin on her broad face, Mrs. Ornelas moves up to the microphone, stating that she has experienced many of the things Mrs. Finch has described. "Many of you know my daughter, Jean. When Jean was around thirteen years old, she told me she was attracted to girls. My initial reaction was shock, although I think deep down inside I always knew the truth. Jean never acted like other girls her age. She wasn't into make-up or any of that girly stuff, and she didn't seem interested in boys. I kept telling myself it was a phase she was going through, that is, until the day Jean told me she liked girls, not boys. Believe me, I was devastated. I remember crying that entire evening. Then when her dad found out, it got worse. He kicked Jean out of the house, saying she was going to contaminate our other daughter. But I stood up for Jean. I insisted she come back home.

After that, things got worse. Jean's dad and I ended up getting a divorce, but there was no way I would ever give up on my daughter. As hard as it was for me to hear it, I spent a lot of time talking with Jean about her true feelings. It was important for Jean to know that I loved her and accepted her. I wouldn't have known how to do this without PFLAG. Being a member of PFLAG also helped me explain Jean's sexuality to her younger sister. Let me tell you, it hasn't been easy. We've had our ups and downs, people have been cruel to us, made hateful remarks, but we've stuck together as a family. I've made it clear to Jean that I will always stand by her. That's all I've gotta say."

The auditorium rumbles with applause as Jean's mom rejoins the other panelists, who take turns complimenting her. When I glance at Jean, I notice her eyes are moist, but she quickly bows her head, pretending to fuss with her sneakers. Moments later, I'm back at the microphone introducing Lance Young, the youngest speaker on our panel. "I'm honored to be here representing LGBT at Laguna University," he begins in a passionate voice. "First, I'd like to describe our goals as an organization. One of our primary objectives is to promote awareness on campus about gay, lesbian and transgendered issues. LGBT strives to foster sensitivity and create a comfortable atmosphere on campus for anyone who is a member of our community. We want our club members to feel more confident about who they are and to know that they are not alone. We also have a Speaker's Bureau composed of members who attend different classes to discuss what it's like to be gay or lesbian. They will often use their own life experiences as examples. Another important objective consists of being active in the local community. We support the local LGBT and are involved in their activities. For example, every year we assist in organizing Gay Pride Day. We also collaborate with the Queer Youth Group, which was recently formed by high school students in the surrounding area. We serve as their mentors and role models. This is extremely important, especially for gay teens, who have some of the highest suicide rates. At the national level, LGBT has been active in getting information out to block discriminatory legislation like Proposition 8 which, as you all know, has denied gays and lesbians the right to marry. We're active in many other ways, such as helping with the nationwide GSA network."

"As for my own personal experience, LGBT has allowed me to fully accept who I am with pride and dignity. When I was in my teens, I was constantly harassed and called names like 'faggot'. I was even beaten up several times and my self-esteem was zero. I actually hated who I was and I often contemplated suicide. It wasn't until I came out and found support systems like LGBT that I was finally able to feel good about myself, to believe that I could go to college one day and make something of myself, and here I am today." Lance pauses for a moment while the audience applauds. "But it's still difficult. You never stop coming out, and you never know how someone will react once they find out you're gay. To this day, my parents don't fully accept me. I still have to be careful about what I say and how I act around them. Nonetheless, I want young people to know that if you're gay or lesbian or transgendered, organizations like LGBT and GSA will help you accept yourself and be proud of who you are. Thank you."

EIGHTEEN

Students applaud loudly when the final speaker of the evening approaches the podium. Smiling, Ms. Martínez says, "Now I know how the Lakers feel at Staples." A few more cheers sound out and Ms. Martínez waits until it is quiet before she addresses the audience. "During my years as a psychologist, I've often had clients who have experienced prejudice and discrimination simply because they are different. Some of my clients are of a different ethnic background, some are gay or lesbian, but at one time or another they have all faced the same type of biased attitudes. As tonight's panelists have indicated, gays and lesbians often hate themselves, have low self-esteem and may even attempt to take their own lives. It's also a fact that hate crimes against gay, lesbian and transgender people have been on the rise, yet, most of these crimes go unreported by the police. For anyone who is Latino, being gay or lesbian is even more traumatic, given their strong Catholic patriarchal family background."

Pausing to take a deep breath, Ms. Martínez continues. "I've never talked about this until today, but I recently found out that my only brother, Andy, was gay. Andy committed suicide when he was a teenager and for all these years, we were led to believe that Andy had taken his life because he was on drugs. I was shocked to find out that Andy took his life, that he chose to commit suicide because he was afraid to tell anyone the truth about his being gay. He couldn't even tell my parents or myself."

The air is thick with silence as Ms. Martínez clears her throat and attempts to steady her voice. Shuffling my feet awkwardly, I think about my own suicide attempt. Mom's suffering. The scars that still seem to make me bleed.

"This is very difficult to talk about," Ms. Martínez, goes on, "especially with my parents. It's a secret my mother kept hidden all these years and even now, she still refuses to bring it out in the open. As Mrs. Finch indicated earlier, parents and families of gay and lesbian students also need support. They need to be informed about their own coming out process, not just that of their children. This is why it is extremely important to inform parents about PFLAG. I recommend that everyone pick up one of Janet's brochures. The last comment I'd like to emphasize, before I conclude for the evening, is that human beings do not choose to be either straight or gay. Most psychologists do not consider sexual orientation to be a conscious choice that can be voluntarily changed. Let me reiterate, homosexuality is not an illness. It does not require treatment and is not changeable. The American Psychological Association, as well as the American Psychiatric Association and every other medical association, strongly insist that sexual orientation is not a choice or something that needs to be treated. Thank you."

As Ms. Martínez returns to her chair, Mrs. Finch pats her on the arm. Back at the microphone, I nervously announce that it is time for the audience to participate with any questions or comments they wish to share. I point out the two mics on both sides of the bleachers for their use. I recognize the first person to approach the microphone, Josiah West, who is president of the Christian Club. "God, our Creator, states in Lev. 18:22, 'Thou shalt not lie with mankind or with womankind. It is an abomination. Homosexuality is a sin.' Several loud boos emerge from the audience, but Josiah ignores them. "Homosexuals were born in sin and they choose this behavior. But God still loves them and will help them change. They only need to ask."

As Josiah returns to his seat, a well-dressed man who looks like a college student addresses the audience from the other microphone. "I'd like to respond to that. I'm gay and I don't think of myself as a sinner. There are millions of gays and lesbians in this country and we don't consider ourselves evil. Anyone who preaches hatred from the Bible, as you are doing, is ill-informed. As Dr. Martínez said, homosexuality is not a choice."

Now a heavy set man, who has been waiting impatiently in line to speak, raises his voice to say, "I'm tired of Christians being portrayed as stupid or ignorant. I am fed up with people who denigrate the word of God. Homosexuals are immoral and they have chosen sinful behavior. That's all I gotta say."

There are several loud boos mixed with a few claps as the loud-spoken man retreats back to his seat. The next person to speak is a gray-haired woman with a young girl at her side, who must be her granddaughter. "I don't understand why people who call themselves Christians have so much hatred and bigotry. I am the proud parent of a son who's gay. He is not a sinner and he is not stupid nor ignorant. He's a successful attorney and I'm very proud of him.

Furthermore, there are all kinds of people in the world, all kinds of religious beliefs, races. I do not understand how so-called Christians can use the Bible to justify hatred against gays and lesbians. Jesus taught us to love everyone, especially those you disagree with."

Another rumble of applause fills the auditorium as the fearless grandma retreats from the microphone. Jean gives me a slight jab on the side when Mrs. Ritter, my Economics teacher from last year, moves up to speak. "I've been a teacher at Roosevelt for almost a decade and I'm here tonight because I want to learn to be more open-minded. Over the years, I've heard both students and teachers using language that is offensive and hurtful when referring to someone who is gay. As a teacher, it's hard to know how to go about confronting students in the classroom when they do this, let alone a colleague in the teacher's lounge. Teachers need to be informed on how to address these issues and I'm glad that our administration is supportive of this forum. I hope we have more like it."

Several students are on their feet cheering loudly as Mrs. Ritter returns to her seat. When Mr. Marshall, the Principal, introduces himself to the audience, Jean and I exchange a look of astonishment. "I'm very pleased that Roosevelt has teachers like Mrs. Ritter, who are supportive of forums such as this one. I'd like to announce that our school administration, with the help of the school district, is already working on modifying Roosevelt's anti-discrimination policy to include sexual orientation. In addition, this summer I will attend a statewide conference on Teaching Tolerance. I've also contacted the Gay Lesbian Straight Educational Network to inquire about mandatory sensitivity training for our teachers and staff. Above all, it's imperative to acknowledge teachers like Brian Miller who are unafraid and willing to take leadership roles with organizations such as the Gay Straight Alliance."

Mr. Marshall's sincere words of support are overshadowed by the next speaker, a burly red-faced man whose comments are forceful and offensive. "Common sense and biology show us that men and women are supposed to have relations with the opposite sex, not the same sex. God made it this way and you need to quit changing the word of God to fit your ignorant beliefs. You can rant and rave all you want about gay rights. Next thing you know, animal rights activists will want to marry their dogs!"

As the angry man abruptly turns around and heads for the exit, someone yells out, "Redneck!" That's all it takes for an argument to break out between the Christian club and the more progressive-minded students.

A distressed Mr. Miller rushes to the podium. It takes several attempts before he can finally quiet the audience and get everyone's attention. "I want to remind everyone that the purpose for holding this forum was not to change anyone's belief system. The objective of tonight's panel discussion has been to create a respectful dialogue so that we can learn to respect our differences. Tonight's forum is not about hateful name-calling and verbal attacks on each other. It is about raising awareness at Roosevelt High School about the importance of creating a safe and comfortable environment for all students. It is our hope to put an end to discrimination of any kind. Thank you all for coming."

NINETEEN
Ms. Martínez

When I walked through the front door, Frank rushed to meet me, an apologetic look on his face. "Lakers won— how did it go?" he asked. Frank had insisted on staying home to watch the Lakers play their archenemy, the Celtics.

Kicking off my shoes, I sank onto the couch. "I think the panel was a huge success, even though some nasty comments that were made at the end, resulting in name-calling between the Christian group and some of the more outspoken university students."

"Well, that's to be expected. How did Tommy do?"

"I am so proud of Tommy. He and Jean Ornelas were poised, confident. They were the perfect moderators."

"I'm glad," Frank replied, adding, "Oh, I almost forgot. Your mom called. She said she left several messages on your cell phone. She wants you to call her before we go to bed. Her voice sounded serious."

Frank's perfect blue eyes studied me. Even after all these years, he was still irresistible. "It's almost nine," I shrugged. "They always go to bed early."

"She said for you to call her no matter what time it was. Who knows, Sandy? Maybe she's ready to talk about your brother."

Feeling heaviness inside, I rose from the couch. "Well, then, I guess I better call her."

As I headed into my office, I thought about what Frank had just said. Maybe Mom *was* ready to break her silence. Several weeks had passed since I'd confronted Mom about Andy's secret. By now, she'd had time to face her anger and confront the truth.

The phone only rang twice before Mom answered it. Hesitating for an instant, I said, "It's me, Mom. I just got home." Thoughts of Dad suddenly entered my mind. He'd been sober for almost a year now. What if he'd gone off the wagon? "Is Dad all right?" I quickly asked.

"Your dad's fine, Sandra."

Sighing with relief, I paused one more time, unsure of my next words. Mom's quivering voice broke the silence. "Sandra, I've been thinking about what you said about Andrés."

"What do you mean?" I blurted out, realizing I knew exactly what Mom meant. This had to be difficult for her, to open up and talk about her feelings. After all, Mom had been raised to be voiceless like most women of her generation. On top of that, to be a woman of color made her even more invisible. Over the years, Sonia and I had often discussed our mothers and their lack of self-empowerment.

I heard a few muffled sobs in the background as Mom continued. "I always knew Andrés was different. From the time he was a little boy, I saw it. I felt it inside."

Now Mom was crying softly into the receiver. "It's okay, Mom. Please don't cry," I gently pleaded, feeling the wetness on my own face while I waited for her to regain her composure.

"I should have said something, done something. But I was so afraid, afraid of what your dad would say, of what people would say. *Hija*, I just didn't have the courage."

As Mom let out another sob, I realized that for the first time in my life, I understood Mom's fears, her confusion, the guilt she'd had to live with all these years. Maya Angelou's words appeared in my thoughts—*If you knew better, you would have done better.* I heard myself whisper, "Mom, it's all right. You did the best you could."

"I never thought Andrés would kill himself because of that. I never imagined it. And then, you know how I was raised Catholic, how they believe only sinners, evil people were like that."

Waves of resentment were surfacing in me again. Even now, after Andy's tragic death, Mom still refused to say the word gay. "Andy was gay, Mom. Gay."

"I know that, Sandra," Mom quietly admitted.

I felt the calmness returning. "Does Dad know?"

"Yes. He kept asking me why I'd gotten so upset with you when you were here, so I finally broke down and told him the whole truth."

I was silent for a moment, imagining Dad's reaction. He had always idealized his only son, put him high on a pedestal. Whispering into the phone, I asked, "How did Dad take it?"

"*Ay, Diosito santo.* He didn't want to accept it at first. He accused me of lying, making it all up. Then he took off to the bedroom, telling me I was acting crazy, but I followed him. I made him listen to me. I told him everything, how I always suspected. Your dad cried—we both did. I think he finally believed me, but he warned me not to tell anyone."

I'd only seen Dad cry once in my life, at Andy's funeral. "Don't worry, Mom. I'll talk to Dad about it, but I'd like to do it in person like I did with Tony Rivera. Tony said it was hard for him, that he always felt guilty for keeping it a secret from us, especially after Andy's death."

"Tony was always such a good friend to Andrés," Mom said, her voice barely a whisper. "We see him all the time with his wife and he always goes out of his way to say hello to us."

Thinking back to the panel and Janet Finch's talk, I said, "You and Dad are both going to need some help. There's an organization called PFLAG, Parents and Friends of Gays and Lesbians—it helps parents cope with their feelings when they find out their children are gay. I can find out if there's a PFLAG in your area."

"I don't know, Sandra," Mom hesitated. "You know how nervous your dad gets talking in front of strangers."

"I know, but what if I take another trip out there and we all go together to the first meeting?"

"*Está bien, hija.* I'll mention it to your dad."

As we hung up the phone, I gazed at the framed photograph of Andy on my desk. It was taken on his thirteenth birthday party and we were hugging and smiling radiantly into the camera. I felt the same happiness as I realized Andy's secret was finally out in the open and we were all free.

TWENTY
Tommy

Tapping on his desk to get everyone's attention, Mr. Miller addresses the GSA club members, "I want to congratulate each of you on the success of last week's forum. If you haven't picked up a copy of today's *Rough Rider*, they ran a great article on the forum and the panelists."

"I read it," Jean interrupts, "It was solid objective reporting."

Marsea and Kayleigh nod in agreement with Jean as Mr. Miller adds, "I know there was a minor scuffle at the end, but I think we handled it well. The important thing is that we have opened up a dialogue about our club's goals. In that regard, we were very successful."

"I almost fainted in class this morning when Judy, from the Christian Club, told me she enjoyed the forum," Rina confesses. "I thought she was going to make some dumb-ass remark—oops, sorry, Mr. Miller."

We all smile, watching Sheena smack Rina on the arm, while Maya and Juanita frown at her. Ignoring all the drama, Mr. Miller goes on, "Mrs. Finch from PFLAG is meeting with Mr. Marshall this week to discuss teacher sensitivity workshops for our staff this summer."

"It's about time!" Rina bellows out in her loud obnoxious voice, and this time Mr. Miller smiles at her candid statement.

"I think we should give ourselves a round of applause," Marsea suggests, ordering Ricki to stop her note-taking. Everyone begins to clap and before I know it, they are chanting my name.

My face is burning as Jean turns to give me an unexpected hug. "*Órale, Señor Presidente*—we did it!"

"I couldn't have done it without you," I reply triumphantly while the club members begin to chant Jean's name.

Once it's quiet again, Mr. Miller explains, "I'd like to make an important announcement before the meeting comes to an end. I've nominated both Jean and Tommy for a Senior Award for their efforts in founding GSA. The banquet is next week."

There are shouts of congratulations as the lunch bell rings and everyone heads for the door. Jean and I exchange a quick glance. Turning to thank Mr. Miller, I admit, "I can't believe it. I've never won an award in my life."

"Me either," Jean repeats, a puzzled look on her face.

Winking at us, Mr. Miller states, "Well, there's always a first time for everything!"

✳ ✳ ✳

During fifth period, I'm floating high in the sky like one of those colorful New Mexican hot air balloons. I'm unable to concentrate, but Mr. Giles doesn't seem to mind since my projects are completed. I can hardly wait to get home so I can tell Mom about the award. Maybe I'll tell Dad, too— he's been a lot nicer since I received the acceptance letter from San Francisco State. Who knows? Maybe Dad will finally accept me for who I am. After all, Mom's been praying like crazy for Dad to come around, and if anyone believes in miracles, it's her.

I'm headed for my locker when I meet up face-to-face with Albert. "Hey, Tommy," he mutters, trying to hurry past me, only I grab him by the arm, forcing him to pause.

"I was hoping I'd see you at our Forum the other night."

"That stuff's not for me," Albert says, his face expressionless like a statue in a museum.

Refusing to let his words discourage me, I ask, "How are things with your parents?"

Albert shifts uncomfortably from one foot to another. "Everything's cool—listen, I have to go or I'll be late for class."

As Albert takes off down the hallway, I call out after him, "Remember—if you ever need a friend, I'm here."

Only Albert doesn't respond. He leaves me standing there feeling like a moron, wondering if I should keep my mouth shut from now on but, like Ms. Martínez said, it's up to Albert to face his own truth.

✳ ✳ ✳

Mario hurries to my side the minute I walk into the classroom. "Look, Tomás," he says in Spanish, holding up his math test. "I got an A!"

"I knew you could do it," I congratulate him, patting him on the head.

"I'm also the Star of the Week. Come see," Mario insists as I follow him to the bulletin board where his photograph is at the center of a huge purple star. There's a mischievous smile on Mario's face and his curly hair is hidden under a Dodger's cap. "Are those your little brothers and sisters?" I ask, gazing at the pictures encircling his photograph.

Mario nods as I recognize Mrs. Guzmán standing next to a man with a thick black moustache. "You look like your dad."

"That's what everyone tells me," Mario proudly admits.

Mr. Sims suddenly appears at our side. "Your tutoring has paid off," he tells me. "Soon Mario won't be needing you. His English is improving every day."

But Mario quickly disagrees with his teacher, insisting that there are words he still doesn't understand. "You have to keep coming," he orders me, as Mr. Sims chuckles.

"Don't worry," I reassure Mario. "You won't get rid of me that easy! Now, what are we working on today?"

Mario's face breaks into a huge smile as he races to his desk for his math book.

✳ ✳ ✳

Mom is in the kitchen preparing enchiladas for dinner when I get home. "Guess what, Mom?" I say, opening the refrigerator door. "Jean Ornelas and I are getting an award for founding the GSA Club."

Pausing for a moment, Mom reaches out to give me a hug. "*Hijo*, I'm so proud of you."

Just then, Amanda comes into the kitchen. Overhearing the good news, she jumps up and down, congratulating me.

María, who is right behind her, says in her whiny pre-teen voice, "It's not like you're going on *American Idol*."

Scolding her, Mom explains, "Tomás is getting an award. See, María, if you study hard like your brother, you might win an award too."

María sticks her ugly tongue out at me while sweet little Amanda says, "I want to be just like you Tommy!"

María rolls her eyes in disgust while I squeeze Amanda tightly.

Over dinner that night, Mom brags about my award to Dad. When he asks what it's for, Mom gets an anxious look on her face, hesitating, but I promptly come to her rescue. "It's for founding the Gay Straight Alliance Club."

There is dead silence. Dad continues eating as if he's not interested in hearing another word from me or Mom. I can feel the anger mounting inside of me. I want to cuss Dad out, tell him he's ignorant and stupid, but Mom's soothing voice snaps me out of it. "I'm really proud of you, *hijo*. You better believe the girls and I will be there the night of the banquet."

Calmly rising from the table, I thank Mom. I don't know how, but she always seems to know the exact words to make me feel better. Screw Dad. Who cares if he goes or not? As Chick Hearn used to say during the Laker games—no harm, no foul.

TWENTY-ONE
Tommy

The night of the Senior Awards Banquet, Mom is pleased to see me wearing a white shirt and tie with dress pants. Amanda sneers at me, arguing that I look as if I'm going to a funeral, but sweet little María insists I'm the handsomest brother in the universe. I give her a giant hug, refusing to let anything ruin my excitement, not even Dad's lame excuse that he can't go because he has to drive his *compadre* to San Martín. His damn loss, I mumble to myself, wondering if he'll even bother to attend my graduation ceremony. Guess I should have learned not to expect anything from him.

By the time we get to the Performing Arts Theater, where the Senior Awards Banquet is being held, it's filled with students and their families. Glancing toward the stage, I make out Mr. Miller talking with another teacher. It's the first time I've seen him dressed in a suit jacket. I'm astounded when I notice Ms. Martínez seated among the counselors and teachers. I had no idea she was going to attend the banquet.

When Jean signals me from the mid-section where she's sitting with her mom, we quickly head in that direction. After I introduce Mom and my sisters to Mrs. Ornelas, Jean and I move to the empty row directly behind them.

"Can you believe it?" Jean complains. "Me wearing a clingy blouse and black pants?"

"You look nice," I compliment her, as Tyrone and his parents come walking through the aisle. I politely greet Mr. and Mrs. Cameron who take the empty seats next to Mom and Mrs. Ornelas.

As Tyrone joins us, I tease him about wearing a tie. Grinning, he replies, "What? You think you're the only one who can get an award?" He then explains that he's receiving a Service award for his work at the Teen Center. "And don't faint, but Rina is getting the Foreign Language Award."

"Now that *is* a miracle!" I exclaim and Jean suddenly grips my arm.

"Look, there's Marsea," she says, pointing toward the front of the room. Just then, Rina appears in the aisle, only Tyrone and I can't help but stare her down, since we've never once seen her in a dress.

"I know," Rina brags, as her Mom joins the other parents, "You don't have to tell me. I look sexy as hell." Then with her usual bluntness, she tells Jean, "*Híjole*, I wouldn't have recognized you."

Jean promptly orders Rina to lower her voice so that we can hear Mr. Grinde's opening remarks. Giving a warm welcome to the audience, Mr. Grinde introduces the principal, Mr. Marshall, who gives a brief summary of why Roosevelt is ranked as one of the top high schools on the Central Coast. Mr. Marshall praises Roosevelt's outstanding students and their achievements. After that, Mr. Marshall invites a retired colonel, who is wearing a U.S. Marine uniform covered with medals, to the podium to announce the military awards. When Jean whispers her disapproval of the military, I have to agree. It seems like every day we hear of another soldier who has died in the Middle East.

The academic awards are the first category of awards to be announced. Candy Hilton receives a thundering applause when she receives the Valedictorian Award. Next come a long list of Honors and Scholarship awards. I'm really happy when Chad Burns is given the Computer Science Award. Everyone's always calling him a geek because he's always on his laptop, but I know they're only jealous because he's so tech savvy.

When they announce the Student Council Awards, we applaud loudly for Marsea, who glides confidently on stage for her certificate. If anyone merits an award tonight, it's Marsea for all her work in Student Government. She's always been at the forefront of issues on our campus. Amid whistles and cheers, Marsea gives an eloquent speech, thanking the teachers as well as the entire student body.

The next category of awards is in Foreign Languages. Once the awards for French and German have been handed out, Mr. Villamil approaches the podium to announce the award for Spanish. A tense look on her face, Rina heads for the stage as soon as she hears her name. Returning to her seat moments later, she holds up her certificate, saying, "Too bad Mosco's not here to see this."

I can feel pin pricks on the back of my neck when Mr. Miller finally approaches the podium. "This year's Leadership awards go to two very special students, Tommy Montoya and Jean Ornelas, for their efforts in organizing Roosevelt's first Gay Straight Alliance Club. At this time, I'd like to introduce Dr. Sandra Martínez, who will present these awards."

Approaching the podium, Ms. Martínez states, "I'm very honored to have been invited to present Roosevelt High School's Leadership awards. The first award goes to Jean Ornelas, who served as Vice President of GSA."

There are loud cheers and clapping as Jean goes onstage for her award. Waiting for the applause to end, Ms. Martínez continues, "And the second Leadership Award is for Tommy Montoya, who served as President of GSA."

My heart thumping, I make my way to the stage, high-fiving Jean as she returns to her seat. As Ms. Martínez hands me my award, she whispers, "I'm very proud of you, Tommy." Whispering thank you, I proudly hold my award above my head. Then I hurry back to my seat where I'm met with more congratulations from Jean, Tyrone and Rina. Mom is crying as she turns around to congratulate me.

When it's Tyrone's turn to go on stage for his award, I overhear Mr. Cameron proudly boast to his wife, "That's my boy!" In that instant, I'm flooded with thoughts of envy, wishing my own dad could've been here, but I quickly push the sadness away. Mom's here and that's all that matters.

As soon as the Sports awards have been handed out, Mr. Grinde closes the evening by thanking all of the parents and their students for their achievements. As people begin to exit the theater, Mr. Miller and Ms. Martínez come by to congratulate our parents. I barely have a chance to introduce Mom to Mr. Miller when Rina interrupts, "Sorry, Tommy. We have to go now. Maya, Rudy, and Ankiza are waiting for us at Tomol Beach."

Apologizing quickly, I turn to Mom, handing her my certificate. "This Award is for you, Mom. You're the one who always taught me to stand tall and be proud."

Mom's crying again as I hurry after Rina and my friends.

TWENTY-TWO
Tommy

At Tomol Beach, we're gathered around the open fire when Maya suddenly jumps to her feet, ordering Tyrone to lower the music. Her voice rising above the rhythmic ocean waves, Maya states, "We'll be graduating soon and this may be the last time we're together as a group. I'd like for each of us to say a few words about our years together at Roosevelt High. I'll go first."

I have to smile to myself. Standing there, ready to lead the way, Maya reminds me of one of the *adelitas* or Soldier Women who fought in the front lines during the Mexican Revolution. "I want you to know that you've been the best of friends since I first came to Roosevelt during my sophomore year. If it hadn't been for your immediate acceptance of me, I would've hated being at a new school. You'll always be my friends, even after graduation." When her voice breaks, Maya signals for Tyrone to go next.

"Don't cry, baby," he whispers, drawing her into his arms for a quick kiss. Tyrone turns to us and says, "I still can't believe I'm going to Laguna University. Like Maya says, we've been there for each other—watched each other's backs all these years. Man, I better stop before I start bawling. That's all I gotta say."

Now it's Rudy's turn to speak. His arms wrapped around Juanita, he begins, "First things first—you're all invited to our wedding." Embarrassed, Juanita gives him a love pinch, as Rudy likes to call it. Wincing, Rudy admits, "Okay, I got it. Like Tyrone and Maya both said—you've been true friends, and you better believe I'm going to make our *raza* proud at Laguna College!"

Calling Rudy conceited, Juanita's face softens as she admits, "*Híjole,* Rudy's right. You've been the best friends anyone could ask for. If it hadn't been for your help that terrible year, I don't think I'd be graduating. Thank you for being there for me. "

There are tears in Juanita's eyes as she and Sheena, who is sitting next to her, exchange a warm glance. We wait as Sheena clears her throat to speak. "I don't even know where to begin. I've learned so much from all of you. Thanks for letting me be part of your group. Because of you, I've changed in ways I never thought I would. So thanks."

Giving Sheena an encouraging tap on the shoulder, Rina doesn't hesitate to speak. "As much as the thought of seeing Rudy again gives me *asco*, I'm excited about Laguna College." When Rudy tries to insult her back, Rina simply orders him to shut up so that she can finish. "You've all been there for me too, even Mosco. I won't forget how we've stuck by each other through all the *mierda*."

Rina's colorful metaphor makes everyone laugh and I suddenly realize I'm even going to miss her truck driver mouth. Marsea is the next one to speak. "You've all been awesome friends. I'll be away at Princeton, but I'll be home during the holiday breaks. Let's plan on having a class reunion."

There are several cheers as we wait for Ankiza to gather her thoughts. Her eyes watery, she begins, "I won't ever forget our Roosevelt High School days—like Rina said, all the times we've been there for each other. If anyone is grateful for that, it's me. I'll be away at USC, but I'll also be coming home for the holidays." Pausing to wipe away the tear sliding down her cheek, Ankiza adds, "You all know where I live."

Now we shift our attention to Jean, who has never hung out with us until tonight. Taking a quick bow, she says, "I personally want to thank each of you for accepting me for who I am—Roosevelt's Unforgettable Lesbian Queen."

While everyone is applauding Jean's flamboyant words, I realize that I'm the last to speak. Studying the familiar faces around me, I confess, "I know that none of us will ever forget our Roosevelt High School days. Like Jean said, you accepted both of us for who we are despite the hateful criticism. You'll never know what that has meant to me. Thank you for being real friends and for standing up for me all these years."

At the sound of these words, Maya rises to her feet again. Demanding we raise our drinks in the air for a toast, she fires away the first cheer, "*¡Qué viva* Roosevelt High*!*"

GLOSSARY

abuelita—dear grandmother.

amá—short for mom.

apá's—short for dad.

asco—disgust, revolution.

así es—That's how it is.

ay, Diosito santo—Oh, my dear Lord .

barrio—Latino/a neighborhood.

Bendícime, Última—first Chicano bestseller by Rudolfo A. Anaya.

Cantinflas—Mario Moreno Reyes, one of Mexico's most famous comedians/actors.

chismosas/os—gossipy persons.

Cinco de Mayo—commemoration of Mexico's victory over the French during the Battle of Puebla in 1862.

comadre/s—female protector; close family friend; a relative of mutual consent, which may not be blood.

compadre/s—male protector; close family friend; a relative of mutual consent, which may not be blood.

corajudo—cranky; moody.

cucaracha—cockroach.

Culture Clash— popular Latino Comedy Troupe composed of three artists, Richard Montoya, Herbert Siguenza and Ric Salinas.

curandera—healer.

de nada—you're welcome.

¡desgraciado!—damn you!

¿dónde andabas?—where were you?

está bien, hija—it's fine, daughter.

¿estás loca?—are you crazy?

Gitano's—belonging to a gypsy.

gordita—form of endearment meaning chubby.

güerita—light-skinned or fair-haired person.

hijo/a—son; daughter.

híjole—Wow! My goodness! Oh, my gosh!

joto—queer; gay.

LGBT—The acronym for Lesbian, Gay, Bisexual and Transgender.

lucha libre—Mexican wrestling.

mal de ojo—folk illness called the "evil eye."

mierda—shit.

mosco/a—literally means a fly.

mujer—woman.

ni modo—Oh, well.

¡órale!—Right on! All right!

pachanga—fiesta or party.

padrino/os—godparent(s); madrina (female godparent).

panza—belly or stomach.

pancita—small belly.

panzón—big-bellied; fatso.

papel picado—a traditional Mexican art form using colorful tissue paper to decorate; often used in Day of the Dead altars.

PFLAG—acronym for Parents and Familes and Friends of Gays and Lesbians.

plogear—to plug in.

¡Qué viva!—Long live!

qué bueno, Tomás—That's good, Tomás.

¿se pelearon otra vez?—Did you get into another argument?

raza—Race; lineage; family; La Raza includes all Latinos regardless of nationality; literally, the Race of the People.

remedios—remedies.

Señor Presidente—Mr. President.

sopapillas—crispy Mexican flatbread deep fried and golden brown.

telenovelas—Spanish soap operas.

tonto—fool.

trucha—that's great/swell; be ready.

vieja, ven—wife, come here.

ya mero, hijo—almost, son.

wáchale—watch out.

Also in the Roosevelt High School Series

Ankiza

Juanita Fights the School Board

Maya's Divided World

Rina's Family Secret

Also in the Roosevelt High School Series

Rudy's Memory Walk

Teen Angel

Tommy Stands Alone

Tyrone's Betrayal

Gloria L. Velásquez created the Roosevelt High School Series "so that young adults of different ethnic backgrounds would find themselves visible instead of invisible. When I was growing up, there weren't any books with characters with whom I could relate, characters that looked or talked like Maya, Juanita, or Ankiza. The Roosevelt High School Series [RHS] is my way of promoting cultural diversity as well as providing a forum for young people to discuss serious issues that impact their lives. I often will refer to the RHS Series as my 'Rainbow Series' since I modeled it after Jesse Jackson's concept of the rainbow coalition."

Velásquez has received numerous honors for her writing and achievements, such as being featured for Hispanic Heritage Month on KTLA, Channel 5, Los Angeles, an inclusion in *Who's Who Among Hispanic Americans, Something About the Author* and *Contemporary Authors*. In 1989, Velásquez became the first Chicana to be inducted into the University of Northern Colorado's Hall of Fame. The 2003 anthology, *Latina and Latino Voices in Literature for Teenagers* and *Children*, devotes a chapter to Velásquez's life and development as a writer. Velásquez is also featured in the 2006 PBS Documentary, *La Raza de Colorado*. In 2007, she was also included in the award-winning anthology *A-Z Latino Writers and Journalists*. In 2004, Velásquez was featured in "100 History Making Ethnic Women" by Sherry Park (Linworth Publishing). Stanford University recently honored her with "The Gloria Velásquez Papers," archiving her life as a writer and humanitarian.